Palestinians, the long history of choosing hate and rejection to a Jewish State

The history of rejectionism

Daniel Farcas

Published by Daniel Farcas, 2024.

This is a work of fiction. Similarities to real people, places, or events are entirely coincidental.

THE HISTORY OF REJECTIONISM

First edition. December 4, 2024.

ISBN: 979-8230142188

Written by Daniel Farcas.

Author: Dr Daniel Farcas
Fellowship
Middle Eastern Studies
Bar Ilan University

Introducción

The Roots of Antisemitism

Antisemitism, one of the longest-standing forms of hatred in human history, has influenced and shaped the treatment of Jewish communities for millennia. From its origins in ancient religious disagreements to its later political and racial dimensions, antisemitism has adapted to the cultural, social, and political contexts of each era. Its persistence is a testament to its ability to evolve, finding new justifications and expressions over time. To understand the full impact of antisemitism, we must examine its historical roots and the ways in which it has affected Jewish identity, resilience, and survival.

Antisemitism is not simply a relic of the past; it is a living, evolving phenomenon. Its foundations lie in theological disputes, political conflicts, and social tensions, but its manifestations have broadened into economic, racial, and cultural prejudices. Tracing its development through key historical epochs sheds light on its enduring relevance and provides context for its modern implications.

Roman Antisemitism: The Genesis of Religious and Cultural Hatred

The origins of antisemitism can be traced back to the Roman Empire, where a profound clash arose between Jewish monotheism and Roman polytheistic traditions. For the Romans, religion was not merely a private matter but a collective civic duty, deeply intertwined with the empire's political and social order. Participation in public rituals and the worship of Roman gods symbolized loyalty to the state. In this context, the Jewish refusal to worship Roman gods or participate in state-sponsored rituals was perceived as a rejection of Roman authority and an act of defiance against the unity of the empire.

Philosopher Bernard-Henri Lévy emphasizes the significance of this tension:

> "The Jewish refusal to worship Roman gods was viewed not only as a religious matter but as a public affront to the power and unity of the Roman Empire."

Theological and Political Threat

The Romans regarded the Jews' distinctiveness as both a theological and political threat. Jewish monotheism, with its strict emphasis on the worship of a single, invisible God, stood in stark contrast to the Roman pantheon, which was rich with deities representing various aspects of life, governance, and the natural world. The Romans saw their gods as integral to the empire's success and security, and any refusal to acknowledge them was seen as a subversive act.

Francisco Gil-White, a historian specializing in ethnic conflicts, elaborates:

> "Jewish monotheism did not merely differ from Roman polytheism; it represented a philosophical challenge. The idea of a single, supreme deity who stood above emperors, states, and armies undermined the ideological foundation of Roman rule."

The Romans, who prided themselves on absorbing and syncretizing the religions of conquered peoples, found Jewish exclusivity baffling and intolerable. Jews refused to adopt Roman gods or allow their God to be portrayed in statues or temples, which Romans considered essential to their religious and political identity.

Luciano Mondino, a political analyst, adds:

"The Jewish refusal to conform to the empire's cultural norms was interpreted not as cultural preservation but as defiance. This perception became a tool for marginalization and, later, outright persecution."

Systematic Suppression of Jewish Identity

The tension culminated in a series of revolts, including the Great Jewish Revolt (66–70 CE) and the Bar Kokhba Revolt (132–135 CE), which led to devastating consequences for the Jewish people. The destruction of the Second Temple in 70 CE by the future Emperor Titus was a turning point. It not only devastated Jewish religious and cultural life but also marked the beginning of a systematic effort to suppress Jewish identity.

Professor Michael Ehrlich of Bar-Ilan University comments:

"The destruction of the Second Temple was not merely a military victory; it was a symbolic assault on the heart of Jewish identity. By targeting their most sacred site, the Romans sought to dismantle the cultural and religious cohesion of the Jewish people."

The Romans escalated their efforts to erase Jewish distinctiveness by banning key practices such as circumcision, Sabbath observance, and Torah study. These prohibitions were designed to strip away the elements that defined Jewish religious and communal life.

Mario Schneider, a remarkable scholar, highlights the impact of these measures:

> "The Roman bans on essential Jewish practices were acts of cultural erasure. They aimed to eliminate the very traditions that sustained the Jewish people through centuries of adversity."

The renaming of Jerusalem to Aelia Capitolina and the establishment of a pagan temple on the Temple Mount further symbolized the Romans' intent to erase Jewish ties to their ancestral homeland.

Financial and Economic Suppression

Shai Farber, a lawyer specializing in terrorism and finance, draws a parallel between Roman economic strategies and modern methods of delegitimization:

> "The Romans imposed heavy taxes, confiscated property, and systematically targeted Jewish economic resources. These measures were an early example of how financial systems can be weaponized to suppress dissenting groups—a tactic that resonates in today's efforts to isolate the Jewish state through economic and political means."

The imposition of the Fiscus Judaicus, a tax levied on Jews throughout the empire to fund the Temple of Jupiter in Rome, was particularly humiliating. It symbolized the subjugation of the Jewish faith to Roman polytheism and marked Jews as a distinct and marginalized group within the empire.

A professor from Ben-Gurion University, an expert on terrorism financing, elaborates:

> "The Roman Empire's financial targeting of the Jewish community established a precedent for using economic pressures to weaken and control minority groups. This model continues to influence modern strategies of delegitimization and economic warfare against the Jewish state."

Legacy of Roman Antisemitism

The Roman suppression of Jewish religious and cultural life had profound long-term consequences. It not only facilitated the Jewish diaspora but also established patterns of antisemitism that persisted through Christian and Islamic societies in later centuries.

Francisco Gil-White explains:

> "The Roman destruction of Jewish identity and dispersal of the Jewish people created a template for antisemitic ideologies. By portraying Jews as a stateless and rebellious group, the Romans laid the groundwork for centuries of exclusion and vilification."

Luciano Mondino adds:
> "The Roman approach to the Jewish question was as much about controlling a minority as it was about defining the empire's identity. The narrative of Jewish incompatibility with broader societal norms has been recycled across centuries and continents."

Shai Farber further emphasizes the modern relevance:
> "The lessons of Roman antisemitism extend beyond history. They remind us how economic and legal frameworks can be manipulated to target and weaken marginalized groups, a tactic that remains alarmingly relevant in contemporary geopolitics."

The Roman period marked the genesis of antisemitism as a systemic phenomenon, intertwining religious, cultural, and economic dimensions. While theological differences initiated the conflict, the Romans' political and social strategies entrenched a pattern of exclusion and vilification. This legacy not only shaped the Jewish experience under Roman rule but also influenced the development of antisemitic ideologies and policies in later civilizations. By understanding this history, we can better recognize and combat the enduring structures of hatred and marginalization.

Distinguishing Antisemitism, Anti-Zionism, and Prejudgment

Prejudgment stems from personal biases or stereotypes, often born of ignorance or misinformation. While harmful, it is generally less organized and lacks the ideological foundation aimed at eradicating a group.

Antisemitism, however, is much more than prejudgment. It is a deeply ingrained ideological framework that positions Jews as scapegoats for society's ills. As Theodor Herzl wrote in Der Judenstaat:

> "Antisemitism is a cancer, not of Jewish existence, but of societies that cannot accept difference. It accuses Jews of being the cause of all suffering, an absurdity as old as it is vile."

Sergio Edelstein captures the societal impact of this hatred:

> "Antisemitism doesn't merely target individuals; it corrodes the moral fabric of societies, perpetuating lies and fear instead of progress."

"It is a result of a world that views our existence as a threat. Only through auto-emancipation, the establishment of our own state, can we hope to escape this endless cycle."

Max Nordau built upon this by emphasizing the need for both physical and moral rejuvenation among the Jewish people:

"The Jewish people, weakened by centuries of exile and persecution, must become strong again—strong in body, strong in spirit. A homeland is not just a refuge; it is the foundation for a new, revitalized Jewish identity."

The Philosophical Roots of Resilience

Ahad Ha'am brought a cultural lens to Zionism, stressing that the Jewish people's survival depended not just on a physical homeland but on a cultural and spiritual revival. For him, the pogroms underscored the urgency of this mission:

"The massacres we endure are not just attacks on our bodies but on our spirit. If we are to survive, we must reclaim our identity—not just as individuals but as a nation bound by shared values and a common destiny."

This vision resonated with thinkers like Einstein, who, though not as a political Zionist, he understood the existential need for Jewish unity:

"The Jewish people, scattered yet unified, have shown a resilience unmatched in history. But resilience alone is not enough; we must also ensure our dignity through collective action and self-determination."

Einstein's critique of antisemitism framed it as a societal illness that could only be cured through education and justice:

"Antisemitism is not just a Jewish problem; it is a human problem. It reveals the moral failings of societies that cannot accept difference. The solution lies in combating ignorance with knowledge and hatred with unity."

The Unique Threat of Antisemitism

Antisemitism stands apart from other forms of prejudice due to its profound and annihilationist nature. Unlike biases that can often be mitigated through education and dialogue, antisemitism transcends misunderstanding. It targets the very essence of Jewish identity and existence, embodying a hatred that is both historical and adaptive. Ahad Ha'am's warning remains hauntingly relevant:

> "Antisemitism does not demand that Jews behave differently; it demands that Jews cease to exist. This is not a critique; it is an annihilationist ideology."

This destructive ideology has persisted across centuries, reappearing in new forms. In recent times, it has been most visibly expressed through the rise of anti-Zionism.

Both antisemitism and anti-Zionism go beyond criticism of individual behavior or state policy. They are existential threats that deny the Jewish people their right to live, thrive, and exist as a nation among nations. Lindembaum concludes:

> "This is not just a Jewish issue; it's a global one. To combat antisemitism is to defend the principles of equality, dignity, and truth for all peoples."

Addressing these threats requires a clear understanding of their unique nature and an unwavering commitment to confronting hatred in all its manifestations.

Building a Future: Lessons from 1881

The events of 1881 catalyzed the Zionist movement, transforming despair into action. Jabotinsky's call for strength and self-defense remains a cornerstone of Jewish resilience:

"The Jewish people must learn that survival requires strength. Weakness invites attack, but strength commands respect."

For Herzl, the solution lay in creating a society that would embody the highest ideals of justice and equality:

"The Jewish state will not only be a refuge for our people but a beacon of hope and peace for the world. It will prove that even the most persecuted people can rise to build a society of dignity and greatness."

The pogroms of 1881 were a turning point that forced the Jewish people to confront the existential threat of antisemitism in all its forms. Zionist leaders responded with a vision that was both practical and philosophical, advocating for self-determination, cultural revival, and strength.

The distinction between antisemitism, anti-Zionism, and prejudgment underscores the unique and insidious nature of hatred against Jews. While prejudgment may stem from ignorance, antisemitism seeks to erase Jewish existence, viewing it as a barrier to societal success or happiness.

The intellectual and practical responses of leaders like Herzl, Pinsker, Nordau, Jabotinsky, and Ahad Ha'am continue to inspire, reminding us that resilience is not just about survival but about reclaiming identity, dignity, and destiny in the face of relentless persecution.

The rise of racial antisemitism in the 19th and early 20th centuries marked a profound shift in the way Jews were perceived in European society. This transformation was largely driven by the advent of pseudoscientific racial theories that classified Jews not just as a religious or cultural group but as a distinct, inferior race. This new form of antisemitism was secular, politically motivated, and deeply intertwined with the growing forces of nationalism and racial ideologies. As Michael Ehrlich observes, "The development of racial theories in the 19th century gave rise to a new form of antisemitism, which no longer saw Jews as a religious or cultural group but as an inferior race."

The racialization of Jews was central to the development of Nazi ideology. Under Adolf Hitler and the Nazi Party, Jews were portrayed as an existential threat to the purity of the Aryan race, fueling the rise of a genocidal movement aimed at their total eradication. Bernard-Henri Lévy highlights this pivotal shift, stating, "The modern world's most persistent and dangerous form of antisemitism is no longer merely rooted in religious intolerance but is deeply entangled with race and politics." The Nazis' propaganda machine, underpinned by deeply racialized antisemitism, depicted Jews not as individuals with diverse backgrounds but as a collective, racially determined enemy that threatened the survival of the German people.

This racialized form of antisemitism reached its horrific apex during the Holocaust, where the Nazi regime's focus shifted from religious identity to racial identity as the justification for the systematic murder of six million Jews. As Lévy further points out, "The Nazi regime did not view Jews as mere enemies of faith but as a subhuman race that needed to be eliminated for the survival of the Aryan race." This ideological shift was responsible for the atrocities of the Holocaust and serves as a grim reminder of the dangers posed by racialized ideologies that reduce individuals to their racial identity rather than their humanity.

The legacy of racial antisemitism continues to influence the world today, as echoes of Nazi racial ideology can be found in various contemporary forms of extremism, which often employ similar narratives about Jews as a racial or existential threat.

Sergio Micco, the former director of the National Institute Against Discrimination in Chile, has spoken about the enduring relevance of understanding antisemitism as a form of racial hatred: "Antisemitism, like all forms of racism, is not only about a history of hatred but about the dangers of continuing to view groups through the lens of race. It is essential to address this prejudice at all levels of society, from education to law enforcement, to prevent its normalization."

Guillermo Holzman, a noted academic on issues of social prejudice, emphasized the role of education in countering antisemitism, stating, "To combat antisemitism, we must educate future generations to recognize the dangerous appeal of racialized hatred and its ability to infect entire societies. History teaches us that the seeds of racial violence are often sown in the classroom."

Ariel Ramírez, a prominent academic reflected on the implications of antisemitism in the modern world: "In today's globalized society, the resurgence of racial antisemitism is not just a Jewish issue; it's a human issue. We must all take responsibility for confronting hate wherever it emerges."

Luciano Mondino, a leading advocate for human rights, further emphasized the need for vigilance in combating racial hatred, saying, "The lessons of the past should never be forgotten. Antisemitism, when racialized, becomes a deadly ideology that undermines the very fabric of human society."

Ricardo Israel Zipper, a political analyst, has pointed out the political dimensions of antisemitism: "Antisemitism is not merely a religious problem, but a political and social issue that affects the stability of societies. It is essential to dismantle these prejudices to foster a peaceful coexistence based on mutual respect and understanding."

Ricardo Brodsky, an academic voice in the discussion of antisemitism, warned that "the persistence of antisemitism, especially in its racialized form, is a reflection of deeper societal fractures. It challenges us to reflect on our values and take concrete steps to address hate in all its forms."

Gabriel Silber, a prominent Jewish figure in Argentina, stated, "Racialized antisemitism is an attack on the very fabric of civilization. It must be confronted through education, dialogue, and the collective will of society to eliminate prejudice and hate."

U.S. Congressman Richie Torres also weighed in on the matter, stating, "Racialized antisemitism isn't just a threat to Jewish people—it's a threat to the very values of democracy, freedom, and equality. We must stand united against any form of hate that seeks to divide us."

U.S. Senator Lindsey Graham, known for his strong stance on international human rights, remarked, "The resurgence of racial antisemitism is a global crisis. We must confront it head-on and ensure that it never again leads to the horrors we witnessed during the Holocaust. The world cannot afford to let such hatred fester."

In conclusion, the persistence of racialized antisemitism underscores the necessity for ongoing education, international cooperation, and the collective will to fight this form of hatred. Figures like Fouling, Ramírez, Mondino, Israel Zipper, Brodsky, Torres, and Graham remind us that antisemitism is not merely a relic of the past but a contemporary danger that demands active resistance from all corners of society. The legacy of racialized antisemitism is a stark reminder of the potential consequences of unchecked hate, making it a crucial issue for the global community to address with urgency and commitment.

Antisemitism in the Modern Era: From the Holocaust to Anti-Zionism

In the post-Holocaust world, antisemitism did not disappear. Instead, it evolved, taking on new forms such as anti-Zionism, which seeks to undermine

The Politics of Rejection: How Palestinian Leadership Repeatedly Denied Peace Offers

For decades, Palestinian leadership has consistently rejected peace proposals, prioritizing conflict over compromise. These rejections, which transcend disputes over borders, signify a denial of Israel's legitimacy and perpetuate suffering for both peoples. The underlying issue is not merely territorial—it's about an unwillingness to recognize the other side's right to exist. This entrenched refusal has not only denied Palestinians the opportunity for peace and self-determination but has also ensured that violence, mistrust, and hardship continue to shape the future of both peoples. As Chilean academic José Joaquín Brunner aptly remarked, "This is not just about borders; it's about an unwillingness to recognize the other side's right to exist. The rejection of coexistence has shaped decades of suffering for all parties involved."

This stance of rejectionism dates back to the very inception of the conflict, as it was crystallized in the 1947 United Nations Partition Plan. The United Nations proposed a solution to the escalating tensions between Jews and Arabs by dividing historic Palestine into two states—one Jewish, one Arab—while establishing Jerusalem as an international city. The Jewish leadership accepted the plan, despite its inherent challenges and limitations. However, the Arab states, including Palestinian leadership, rejected the plan outright, refusing to acknowledge the legitimacy of a Jewish state in the region. This rejection was not only a refusal to share the land but a rejection of the

Jewish people's right to self-determination. This marked the beginning of a pattern: a refusal to negotiate or coexist peacefully with Israel.

Israeli Prime Minister Golda Meir famously remarked, "Peace will come when the Arabs love their children more than they hate us," encapsulating the core of the Palestinian rejectionist mindset. In Meir's view, peace would only become possible when Palestinian leadership valued the future of their children more than the ideological opposition to the Jewish state. However, this perspective has consistently been sidelined by the Palestinian leadership's desire for territorial and ideological dominance, at the cost of peace and stability.

In 1967, this rejectionist mentality was reaffirmed by the Arab League's "Three No's" declaration in Khartoum: "No peace with Israel, no recognition of Israel, no negotiations with Israel." This declaration served as the framework for Palestinian policy throughout much of the 20th century, with Palestinian leadership continuing to reject peace offers on the basis that they would be seen as a form of recognition of Israel's right to exist. It was not about peace with Israel; it was about erasing Israel altogether, a belief that has sustained Palestinian rejectionism into the present day.

—-

Camp David Accords (1978): The Path Not Taken

One of the first opportunities for a historic breakthrough in the Arab-Israeli conflict came in 1978, when U.S. President Jimmy Carter mediated the Camp David Accords between Israel and Egypt. The accords culminated in a peace agreement between Israel and Egypt, the first such agreement between Israel and an Arab nation. The peace treaty included the return of the Sinai Peninsula to Egypt and the recognition of Israel's right to exist, marking a critical turning point in the Arab-Israeli conflict.

However, Palestinian leadership, under the Palestine Liberation Organization (PLO) and its leader Yasser Arafat, refused to participate in the Camp David talks. This marked a missed opportunity for the Palestinians to be part of a transformative agreement that could have paved the way for peace and stability in the region. Spanish activist Ángel Mas criticized this refusal, stating, "When presented with the chance to be part of a transformative agreement, Palestinian leaders chose absence over engagement." This act of omission effectively sidelined the Palestinian cause at a time when Arab-Israeli relations were moving toward normalization. Former Chilean President Ricardo Lagos added, "Camp David was a milestone, but the Palestinians' refusal to engage showed their unwillingness to embrace meaningful progress."

At the same time, the rejection of peace talks served to further entrench the notion that Palestinian leadership would rather hold onto a narrative of victimhood and resistance than work toward a pragmatic resolution. This refusal would set the stage for future failures in the peace process, as Palestinians chose ideological purity over practical solutions.

Camp David Summit (2000): From Hope to Violence

The year 2000 saw another potential turning point in the Israeli-Palestinian conflict with the Camp David Summit, convened by U.S. President Bill Clinton, Israeli Prime Minister Ehud Barak, and Palestinian Authority President Yasser Arafat. At this summit, Israel offered a comprehensive peace plan that included nearly all of the West Bank and Gaza Strip, shared control over Jerusalem, and compensation for Palestinian refugees. This was an unprecedented offer, and one that would have fundamentally reshaped the region.

However, once again, Palestinian leadership rejected the offer outright. Arafat, despite the generosity of the proposal, refused to make a deal, and instead, launched the Second Intifada, a violent uprising that resulted in the deaths of thousands of Israelis and Palestinians. The violent escalation that followed was a stark reminder that Palestinian rejectionism was not a tactical negotiation stance but rather a profound ideological commitment to eradicating Israel as a Jewish state.

Clinton lamented the missed opportunity, saying, "Arafat missed the opportunity of a lifetime. The offer was generous, and yet the answer was violence." Israeli Knesset member Einat Wilf emphasized the tragic consequences of this rejection, stating, "Arafat's refusal was not a negotiation tactic; it was a clear statement that no offer could ever satisfy the demand to erase Israel." Prominent thinker Bernard-Henri Lévy echoed this sentiment: "The rejections are not about borders—they are about erasing Israel from the map. Until this changes, peace will remain elusive."

The violence that followed Arafat's rejection of the Camp David summit would lead to a period of heightened tension, with further terror attacks, retaliations, and a worsening humanitarian situation. This cycle of violence only deepened the divisions between Israelis and Palestinians, further complicating the peace process.

—-

Hamas and the Politics of Violence

The rise of Hamas, an Islamist political and militant organization, further entrenched Palestinian rejectionism. Founded in 1987 during the First Intifada, Hamas rejects Israel's existence entirely and seeks to replace Israel with an Islamic state. As a designated terrorist organization by many countries, including the United States, European Union, and Israel, Hamas has used violence as a tool to achieve its goals, regularly targeting Israeli civilians through suicide bombings, rocket fire, and other forms of terrorism.

U.S. Senator Marco Rubio condemned Hamas's actions, stating, "Hamas doesn't care about the Palestinian people. They use civilians as human shields while spending resources on rockets instead of schools and hospitals." Israeli historian Aviv Gur emphasized the destructive influence of Hamas, stating, "Hamas thrives on conflict and chaos. Their refusal to recognize Israel and their glorification of violence ensure that Palestinians remain trapped in suffering." Hamas's rejectionist ideology has cemented itself as an obstacle to any meaningful peace process, ensuring that peace remains out of reach for both Israelis and Palestinians.

Many thinkers, including Bernard-Henri Lévy, reject Hamas's ideology, viewing it as an insurmountable barrier to peace. Lévy stated, "Hamas is not a resistance movement—it is an instrument of hatred and destruction, and it has no place in the future of a peaceful Middle East."

—-

Modern Opportunities: The Abraham Accords and Beyond

The Abraham Accords, signed in 2020, marked a historic moment in Middle Eastern diplomacy. The agreements, which normalized relations between Israel and several Arab nations, including the United Arab Emirates, Bahrain, Sudan, and Morocco, demonstrated that peace and cooperation were achievable when leaders embraced pragmatism over ideological rigidity. These accords were a signal that Arab-Israeli peace was no longer an impossible dream, and that progress was possible even in the absence of Palestinian leadership's cooperation.

Despite the positive momentum generated by the Abraham Accords, Palestinian leadership denounced the agreements, choosing instead to hold onto outdated narratives of victimhood and rejection. Israeli lawmaker Sharren Haskel criticized their reaction, stating, "While Arab states moved forward, Palestinian leaders clung to a destructive narrative of victimhood and rejection." Former U.S. Secretary of State Mike Pompeo commented, "The Abraham Accords show that peace is possible when leaders prioritize progress over politics. The Palestinians' refusal to engage reflects a tragic inability to see beyond their grievances."

The rejection of the Abraham Accords was not just a missed opportunity; it was a clear signal that Palestinian leadership, especially under the influence of groups like Hamas, remained deeply committed to maintaining a culture of rejectionism, rather than seeking constructive solutions.

—-

A Call for Leadership

The refusal of Palestinian leadership to accept peace proposals has perpetuated cycles of violence and suffering, not just for Palestinians but for Israelis as well. Global leaders have repeatedly emphasized the need for Palestinian leadership to recognize Israel's right to exist and to embrace the possibility of coexistence. Former Argentine President Mauricio Macri summarized the global frustration, stating, "The path to peace is clear—it requires acceptance, recognition, and the courage to compromise. The question is whether Palestinian leaders are willing to take it."

Israeli politician Einat Wilf posed a stark reality, stating, "Until the Palestinian leadership is willing to abandon rejectionism and embrace coexistence, there will be no peace for their people—or for Israelis." The words of Shimon Peres, former Israeli president and peace advocate, serve as a poignant reminder: "The Palestinians never miss an opportunity to miss an opportunity." Unless this cycle of rejectionism ends, peace will remain an elusive dream for both nations.

Chapter 2: The Ideology of Rejectionism

—-

At the heart of Palestinian rejectionism lies not merely opposition to Israeli policies but a fundamental denial of Israel's right to exist as a Jewish state. This ideological stance, deeply rooted in political, religious, and cultural beliefs, has become a cornerstone of Palestinian nationalism and Arab identity for generations. Rejectionism transcends the rejection of specific peace proposals; it reflects an unwavering refusal to accept Israel's legitimacy as a sovereign state and the historical and religious connections of the Jewish people to the land. This refusal has shaped the trajectory of the Israeli-Palestinian conflict for decades, rendering meaningful progress toward peace elusive.

The Nature of Rejectionism

Einat Wilf emphasizes the depth of this problem: "Palestinian rejectionism is not about borders or settlements. It is about the very idea that a Jewish state has a right to exist in any borders. Until this changes, peace will remain elusive." This entrenched ideology manifests in public statements, political rhetoric, education systems, and cultural narratives, where Israel's existence is portrayed as illegitimate and its destruction as a desirable goal.

This is not merely a stance held by extremist groups like Hamas, whose charter explicitly calls for Israel's annihilation. It permeates broader Palestinian society and leadership, including the Palestinian Authority (PA). Leslie Klaff, an expert on antisemitism, highlights how "rejectionism is the product of a cultivated narrative that denies Jewish historical and cultural ties to the land while glorifying 'resistance' in forms that often justify violence and terror."

Leadership and the Perpetuation of Rejectionism

Palestinian leadership plays a pivotal role in perpetuating rejectionism. While Hamas is overt in its hostility, the Palestinian Authority employs more subtle but equally damaging tactics. PA-sanctioned media, textbooks, and public statements often delegitimize Israel and deny Jewish ties to Jerusalem and the broader region. Gabriel Zaliasnik, a Chilean Jewish leader, observes, "What is most troubling is the normalization of rejectionism at all levels of Palestinian governance. Even peace agreements are treated not as steps toward coexistence but as tools of temporary advantage."

Tzipi Livni, former Israeli Foreign Minister and lead negotiator in peace talks, has firsthand experience with the challenges of Palestinian rejectionism. She explains: *"Throughout negotiations, it became clear that the issue was not borders or settlements but a refusal to recognize Israel.

The Role of the Mufti: A Historical Foundation

The influence of rejectionism in Palestinian political thought can be traced back to some of the earliest leaders of Palestinian nationalism. One of the most influential figures in this regard was Haj Amin al-Husseini, the Grand Mufti of Jerusalem during the British Mandate period. Al-Husseini played a crucial role in fostering anti-Jewish sentiment in the region, particularly in opposition to Jewish immigration and the idea of establishing a Jewish homeland in Palestine. His leadership, during a time when tensions between Jews and Arabs were intensifying, helped solidify the idea that the presence of a Jewish state in Palestine was unacceptable.

In the 1930s and 1940s, al-Husseini's leadership catalyzed violent uprisings against Jewish immigration, and he promoted the idea that Palestine must remain an exclusively Arab territory. His opposition to the establishment of a Jewish state was not limited to political concerns but extended to existential, cultural, and religious factors. Al-Husseini was a vocal advocate for the Arab world's resistance to the Zionist project, which he saw as a foreign, colonial imposition on the Arab people. His deep animosity toward Jews was further amplified by his collaboration with Nazi Germany during World War II, which solidified his anti-Semitic views and reinforced his stance that Jews had no place in Palestine or the Arab world.

Bernard-Henri Lévy, a French philosopher and political theorist, argues that the Mufti's ideological stance laid the groundwork for Palestinian rejectionism:

> "The Mufti's rejection of the Jewish people's right to exist in Palestine has lived on in the form of modern Palestinian rejectionism. It is not simply about land; it is about the denial of Jewish sovereignty."

Lévy's perspective underscores the idea that rejectionism goes beyond territorial disputes. It is about challenging the fundamental legitimacy of Jewish existence in the region, a theme that continues to define much of the Palestinian national discourse today. Al-Husseini's collaboration with Nazi forces and his quest to deny Jews any place in the Middle East had a profound impact on the ideological development of Palestinian nationalism. His legacy continues to influence Palestinian leaders, who follow his rejectionist approach to the Israeli-Palestinian conflict.

The Role of Religious Ideology and Hamas

In modern times, the most prominent embodiment of rejectionism has been Hamas, the Islamist militant group that controls the Gaza Strip. Founded in 1987, Hamas has become a dominant force in Palestinian politics, and its ideological roots are firmly entrenched in a radical Islamic framework. Hamas is driven by the belief that Palestine is an Islamic waqf, a religious endowment that cannot be ceded to non-Muslims, and that the land must remain under Muslim rule forever. Hamas does not view the Israeli-Palestinian conflict as a political struggle, but rather as a religious and existential war between Islam and Judaism.

Hamas's charter, established in 1988, explicitly calls for the destruction of the state of Israel and rejects any negotiations with the Israeli government. Hamas's founders believed that Israel's existence was a violation of Islamic principles and that any peace agreement with Israel was not only unthinkable but heretical. This rejectionism is based on the belief that the Jewish presence in the land of Palestine is illegitimate and that the land is an Islamic inheritance, which must be defended at all costs.

Aviv Gur, an Israeli political analyst, captures the essence of Hamas's position:

> "Hamas is not interested in peace; they are interested in the obliteration of the state of Israel. Their ideology is rooted in the belief that any form of peace with Israel is heretical."

Hamas's rejectionism is totalizing and absolute. They do not seek compromise or negotiation but instead adhere to an uncompromising vision in which Israel must be destroyed. Hamas's approach contrasts sharply with that of the Palestine Liberation Organization (PLO), which in the past has expressed willingness to negotiate with Israel and accepted the possibility of a two-state solution. While the PLO's stance has evolved over time to embrace negotiations and recognize Israel's existence, Hamas has steadfastly maintained that any form of peaceful coexistence is anathema to its religious and ideological worldview.

In this sense, Hamas represents the purest form of rejectionism within Palestinian politics. The movement views Israel's existence as a direct challenge to its religious and political ideology, and any attempt to find a peaceful resolution to the Israeli-Palestinian conflict is seen as an act of betrayal to Islam. Hamas's power and influence in Gaza have made it an intractable obstacle to peace, as its ideology remains diametrically opposed to any form of recognition of Israel.

Arab Leaders' Support for Rejectionism

The influence of rejectionism extends beyond Palestinian leaders and has been perpetuated by various Arab leaders throughout the 20th and 21st centuries. Many Arab regimes have used the Palestinian cause as a tool to rally their populations and unite them against a common enemy—Israel. These leaders have played a significant role in perpetuating the narrative that any peace with Israel would be a betrayal of Palestinian rights and Arab identity.

One of the most prominent examples of this rejectionist attitude was Gamal Abdel Nasser, the former President of Egypt, who played a pivotal role in shaping Arab policy toward Israel. Nasser famously stated:

> "We will never accept the partition of Palestine. There can be no peace as long as Israel exists."

This statement encapsulates the stance of many Arab leaders during the mid-20th century, who refused to recognize the legitimacy of the Israeli state. Nasser, who was a leading figure in the Arab nationalist movement, saw the creation of Israel as a direct affront to Arab unity and sovereignty. His refusal to accept the legitimacy of the Israeli state was rooted in both political and ideological concerns, as he believed that Israel's existence undermined the pan-Arab dream of a united Arab world. Nasser's stance resonated deeply with many Arabs, and his rejection of Israel served as a model for future Arab leaders, even after the peace treaty between Egypt and Israel in 1979.

While Egypt's peace treaty with Israel marked a significant shift in the region, many Arab countries continued to resist recognizing Israel. The rejection of Israel was not just a Palestinian position but a broader Arab stance that became embedded in the collective consciousness of the Arab world. Arab leaders used the Palestinian cause as a means of mobilizing their populations, framing the struggle as a symbol of resistance to Zionism, imperialism, and Western influence.

This ideological stance continued into the 21st century, with many Arab leaders still refusing to normalize relations with Israel. Even as some Arab countries, such as Egypt, Jordan, and more recently the United Arab Emirates and Bahrain, have signed peace agreements with Israel, others remain steadfast in their refusal to recognize Israel's right to exist. The rejectionist ideology has thus remained a key obstacle to broader peace in the region.

Global Perspectives on Rejectionism

Rejectionism is not only a Palestinian or Arab issue—it has profound global implications. Many international political figures and analysts have weighed in on the impact of Palestinian rejectionism on the broader peace process. Some have emphasized that the refusal to recognize Israel's legitimacy is a central obstacle to any lasting peace in the Middle East.

Gabriel Silber, a prominent expert on Middle Eastern politics, argues that the persistence of Palestinian rejectionism is not merely an issue between Israelis and Palestinians but is part of a broader regional and global problem:

> "The perpetuation of Palestinian rejectionism remains a central obstacle to peace. It is not merely an issue between Israelis and Palestinians; it is a question of the broader Arab and Islamic world's stance on Israel's right to exist."

British Labour politician Ian Wilf echoes this sentiment:
> "For peace to have a chance, Palestinian leadership must acknowledge the legitimacy of Israel, not just as a political entity, but as the homeland of the Jewish people."

These voices stress the importance of mutual recognition in the pursuit of peace. Without recognition of Israel as a legitimate Jewish state, no meaningful peace process can occur. Palestinian rejectionism, in this context, is not just a political issue but a fundamental existential challenge to Israel's right to exist.

In response to the ongoing rejectionism, former Spanish Prime Minister Felipe González emphasizes:
> "Peace cannot be achieved when one side rejects the very foundation of the other's existence. Palestinian rejectionism has proven to be a recurring barrier to any genuine negotiation process."

Similarly, former Israeli Prime Minister Ehud Olmert reflects on the challenge that rejectionism poses to peace:
> "You cannot negotiate with someone who denies your right to exist. It is an existential challenge for Israel, and one that cannot be overcome through negotiations alone."

These perspectives reflect the global consensus that until Palestinian leadership accepts Israel's right to exist, the prospects for lasting peace remain distant. Rejectionism is not merely an ideological position; it is a fundamental obstacle to resolving the Israeli-Palestinian conflict and achieving peace in the region.

Chapter 3: The Mufti and the Legacy of Rejection

The legacy of Haj Amin al-Husseini, the Grand Mufti of Jerusalem, has profoundly shaped Palestinian political thought and continues to reverberate through the decades. His uncompromising rejection of Jewish self-determination and vehement opposition to Jewish immigration into Mandatory Palestine became central tenets of Palestinian nationalism and rejectionism.

Al-Husseini's ideological stance was not merely political; it was deeply rooted in a denial of the historical and religious ties of the Jewish people to the land. This denial underpinned his collaboration with Nazi Germany during World War II, where his efforts extended to spreading anti-Semitic propaganda and advocating against the resettlement of Jewish refugees in Palestine. As philosopher Bernard-Henri Lévy has noted:

> "The Mufti's collaboration with Hitler was not just a political maneuver; it was a fundamental denial of the Jews' historical and religious ties to the land. His actions laid the groundwork for the rejection of any form of compromise with Israel."

Michael Ehrlich delves further into the ideological underpinnings of this rejectionism:

> "The Mufti's opposition to Zionism was not just a resistance to a political project but an outright denial of Jewish history and identity. His narrative sought to erase the millennia-long connection of the Jewish people to the land, creating a framework of rejection that has persisted in Palestinian politics."

Zionism itself, as articulated by its founders, was always about the re-establishment of a Jewish homeland in the land of Israel, not a colonialist enterprise. Theodor Herzl, the father of modern political Zionism, stated:

> "The Jews who wish it will have their state. We shall live at last as free men on our own soil, and die peacefully in our own homes." (The Jewish State, 1896)

Chaim Weizmann, a central figure in the Zionist movement, also emphasized the legitimacy and moral necessity of Jewish self-determination:

> "We are not asking for more land. We are asking for the land which is our own, our home, the land where we belong, and where we have the right to live and to flourish." (Speech at the Zionist Congress, 1931)

Weizmann was also clear about the necessity of Jewish sovereignty for the survival of the Jewish people, reflecting on the painful history of Jewish persecution and the urgent need for a secure homeland:

> "The Jews have been scattered all over the world, but wherever they have been, they have been subject to persecution, to injustice, to degradation. We seek not only a place to live but a place where the Jewish soul can thrive and express itself freely." (Letter to Lord Balfour, 1917)

Steven Pinker, a cognitive scientist and historian, explains the deep-seated historical significance of Zionism in shaping Jewish self-determination:

> "Zionism is the Jews' return to their historic homeland, not an imperialist project. It's about the survival and flourishing of a people who had been scattered across the world for millennia, often persecuted, and without a place to call their own." (The Better Angels of Our Nature, 2011)

Einat Wilf emphasizes how this ideological divide has affected the prospects for peace:

> "The Mufti established a dangerous precedent where rejecting any compromise was seen as a form of loyalty to the cause. This has trapped Palestinian leaders in a cycle of refusing peace proposals, even those that offered substantial concessions, out of fear of appearing disloyal to the narrative of rejection."

Shareen Hazzelel, an Israeli political analyst, reflects on the historical context and impact of the Mufti's actions:

> "The Mufti's legacy remains central to understanding the nature of Palestinian rejectionism. His denial of Jewish history and the creation of a myth of Palestinian victimhood that excludes any form of Jewish connection to the land has set the stage for the ongoing refusal to recognize Israel's legitimacy." (The Politics of Rejection, 2020)

Hazzelel further discusses how Palestinian leadership has internalized this narrative:

> "For Palestinian leadership, negotiating peace with Israel means rejecting the fundamental pillar of their identity—the notion that they are the rightful heirs of the land. This has made it nearly impossible for them to acknowledge the existence of a Jewish state without losing their political legitimacy."

Haviv Rettig Gur notes the enduring impact of the Mufti's framing of the conflict:

> "By presenting Zionism as an imperialist and illegitimate project, the Mufti gave Palestinian rejectionism a moral justification that persists to this day. This framing has allowed the rejection of peace deals to be seen not as failures but as acts of resistance."

Levi Eshkol, Israel's third Prime Minister, reflected on the consequences of this ideology in the wake of the Six-Day War:

> "The tragedy of Palestinian leadership is their inability to move beyond rejectionism. Again and again, they have chosen the path of refusal, leaving both peoples trapped in conflict when peace could have been within reach."

The Mufti's influence cannot be overstated. He reframed the Zionist movement as a colonialist project, portraying the Jewish presence in the Middle East as an affront to Arab and Islamic identity. This worldview, which equated Zionism with imperialism and illegitimacy, became the ideological backbone of Palestinian resistance and rejectionism.

As Kenneth M. Mending aptly summarizes:

> "The tragedy of Palestinian rejectionism is not just its failure to achieve peace but its success in perpetuating a conflict that could have been resolved decades ago. The Mufti's ideology laid the foundation for this enduring cycle of denial and destruction."

The enduring impact of al-Husseini's rejectionism highlights a central challenge in the pursuit of peace: the deeply entrenched narratives that frame compromise as betrayal. Understanding this legacy is crucial to addressing the barriers that continue to impede a resolution to the Israeli-Palestinian conflict.

Chapter 4

Palestinian Terror Attacks: Murders, Kidnappings, and International Terrorism

The history of Palestinian violence against Jews is not limited to localized attacks within the borders of Israel, but has grown into a global phenomenon. The use of terror as a weapon, targeting both Israeli civilians and international Jewish communities, has been a strategy adopted by various Palestinian factions over decades. These attacks, deeply rooted in both -political struggles and religious extremism, have caused immeasurable pain and left an indelible mark on the Jewish people.

Terror Attacks and Murders

The escalation of Palestinian violence can be traced back to the early stages of the Israeli-Palestinian conflict, with a significant surge in terrorism during the Second Intifada (2000-2005). The violence peaked with the increase in suicide bombings, rocket attacks, and shootings that indiscriminately targeted Israeli civilians. The bombings, in particular, were aimed at places of everyday life — buses, cafes, shopping centers — and often resulted in large-scale casualties. During the height of the Intifada, Palestinian groups such as Hamas and Palestinian Islamic Jihad (PIJ) orchestrated numerous attacks aimed at causing maximum civilian harm.

For example, the Dolphinarium discotheque bombing in Tel Aviv in 2001, which claimed the lives of 21 Israeli teenagers, is a tragic illustration of this era. The target was a civilian social space, with the intention not only to kill but to send a message that no place was safe for Israelis. Lesley Klaff notes, "These attacks reflected the evolution of Palestinian terror tactics, which increasingly focused on inflicting psychological and social damage rather than just military defeat." Attacks on civilian targets were intended to break the Israeli public's spirit, incite fear, and destabilize the social fabric of the country.

The Munich Olympics Massacre of 1972, carried out by Black September, is another example of Palestinian terrorism targeting Jews on the world stage. Eleven Israeli athletes were taken hostage and ultimately murdered by the Palestinian terror group. The act of terror, carried out on foreign soil, not only shocked the world but underscored how deeply Palestinian violence was intertwined with a broader ideology aimed at targeting Jews wherever they could be found. Michael Ehrlich remarks, "This attack exemplified the global ambitions of Palestinian terror groups, showcasing how violence against Jews transcended national borders and sought to strike at the heart of Israeli identity."

Kidnappings and Hostage Situations

Kidnapping Israeli soldiers and civilians has long been a tactic of Palestinian terrorism. Kidnapping serves multiple purposes: it creates leverage for future negotiations, generates widespread media attention, and, often, forces Israeli leadership into difficult decisions. One of the most infamous kidnappings in modern history was the abduction of Israeli soldier Gilad Shalit by Hamas in 2006. Shalit was captured during a cross-border raid and held captive for over five years in Gaza, during which time he became a symbol of Palestinian resistance. Hamas used his captivity to demand the release of hundreds of Palestinian prisoners, many of whom were involved in terrorism.

The Shalit case is a stark example of how hostage-taking has become a central part of the Palestinian terror playbook. The kidnapping and subsequent five-year ordeal of Gilad Shalit galvanized public opinion in Israel and around the world, as Israel ultimately agreed to a controversial prisoner exchange, releasing over 1,000 Palestinian prisoners in exchange for Shalit's freedom. This exchange underscored the broader strategic use of kidnapping, not just as a military tool, but as a form of psychological warfare. As Lesley Klaff explains, "The emotional and political leverage generated by kidnapping goes far beyond the act of violence itself — it becomes a symbol of Palestinian resistance and a bargaining chip on the international stage."

Another example of kidnapping and murder occurred in 2014, when three Israeli teenagers — Naftali Fraenkel, Gilad Shaar, and Eyal Yifrach — were abducted by Hamas militants in the West Bank. The three teenagers were ultimately found murdered, and their deaths sparked an Israeli military operation to capture the perpetrators and quell growing violence. This act of abduction, followed by murder, highlighted the continued use of terror and violence in Palestinian resistance, as well as the brutal reality faced by Israeli civilians living near conflict zones.

The Role of Antisemitism in Palestinian Terrorism

At the core of Palestinian violence is a pervasive and long-standing antisemitic ideology that views Jews not merely as political adversaries but as a central enemy. Bernard-Henri Lévy has observed, "The narrative of the Jews as an existential threat is embedded in the rhetoric and actions of Palestinian terror organizations. It is not just about a territorial dispute but a deep-seated hatred that dehumanizes Jews as a people."

In many cases, Palestinian terrorist groups have conflated the political struggle over the land with broader religious and racial animus toward Jews. The portrayal of Jews as subhuman, invaders, and enemies of Islam has been propagated through Palestinian media, education, and political speeches. Michael Ehrlich elaborates, "Palestinian violence is often not just about expelling Israelis from the West Bank or Gaza; it's about confronting Jews as a people, rooted in deep-seated hatred rather than a pragmatic political conflict."

This deeply entrenched antisemitism is not just a product of the Israeli-Palestinian conflict but reflects a broader regional attitude toward Jews. As Lesley Klaff writes, "Palestinian violence is not an isolated response to Israel's policies; it is a manifestation of a culture that, at its roots, promotes the denial of Jewish identity and legitimacy." These beliefs are reflected in the incitement to violence seen in Palestinian schools, textbooks, and media, where Jews are often depicted as enemies of Islam and humanity. The terrorism carried out by groups like Hamas is therefore not merely a political strategy but an extension of an ideology that seeks to eliminate Jewish presence, both in Israel and in the broader region.

The Palestinian Authority (PA) has been widely criticized for its practice of paying salaries to individuals who have committed acts of terrorism, including those who have murdered Jews. This policy, often referred to as the "pay-for-slay" program, provides financial compensation to Palestinians convicted of terrorism-related offenses, including those involved in attacks against Israeli civilians and soldiers. These payments have been a point of contention for many in the international community, as they are seen as a direct form of support for violence and a reinforcement of the culture of incitement and hatred.

The PA has defended the practice, claiming it is a form of social welfare and compensation for families of "martyrs" and prisoners. However, critics argue that by paying terrorists and their families, the PA is incentivizing violence and promoting a cycle of hatred. As U.S. Senator Lindsey Graham stated, "Paying terrorists for killing innocent people is not just morally wrong—it encourages further acts of terror. The international community must hold the Palestinian Authority accountable for this dangerous policy."

Israel's Prime Minister Benjamin Netanyahu has also condemned the practice, saying, "The Palestinian Authority's payment to terrorists who murder Jews is a direct incitement to violence. It is a policy that not only undermines peace but also emboldens those who seek to destroy Israel."

In addition, the U.S. Congress has passed laws, such as the Taylor Force Act, which cuts off U.S. aid to the PA if it continues to fund these payments. U.S. Senator Marco Rubio remarked, "By continuing to pay terrorists, the Palestinian Authority is sending a message that terrorism is rewarded. This must end for any meaningful peace to be achieved."

The practice has drawn strong condemnation from various international human rights organizations, including the United Nations, which have called for the cessation of such payments. Human Rights Watch has criticized the PA for using its resources to incentivize violence, saying, "The Palestinian Authority's support for terrorism and its use of public funds to reward violent acts against civilians is incompatible with international law."

Despite international pressure, the PA has continued this policy, reflecting its broader approach to the Israeli-Palestinian conflict, which often involves promoting anti-Israel sentiment and justifying violent resistance against what it perceives as Israeli occupation.

In response, figures such as former French President Nicolas Sarkozy have emphasized the need for a shift in Palestinian leadership, stating, "A true path to peace will never be achieved while the Palestinian Authority continues to reward violence. This policy must end for any hope of reconciliation to take root."

Mario Schneider, a well-respected academic voice in the field of Middle Eastern and Israeli studies, has added, "The PA's continued payments to terrorists is a dangerous precedent. It sends a message that violence against Jews is not only acceptable but rewarded, making the path to peace even more elusive."

Eduardo Frei Ruiz-Tagle, former President of Chile, expressed his concern, stating, "The Palestinian Authority's practice of financially rewarding terrorists undermines any effort toward a peaceful resolution in the region. This policy promotes a culture of hate and violence, and it is essential for the international community to act to stop it."

In summary, the Palestinian Authority's policy of paying salaries to individuals who commit acts of terrorism, including the murder of Jews, remains a significant obstacle to peace, as it directly promotes and incentivizes violence while hindering efforts to build trust between Israelis and Palestinians. The continued support for this policy by the PA demonstrates the complexities and challenges surrounding the Israeli-Palestinian conflict and its broader international implications.

The long-standing impact of these ideologies is clear in the frequent eruption of violence and terror against Jews, which is often fueled by the belief that Palestinians are engaged in a religious war against the Jewish people. The antisemitic rhetoric that dominates much of the Palestinian political discourse is both a cause and a consequence of the continuing cycle of violence, illustrating how hatred can be passed down from one generation to the next, perpetuating the tragic conflict between Jews and Palestinians.

The Long Legacy of Palestinian Terrorism and Antisemitism

Palestinian terrorism, encompassing kidnappings, murders, and targeted attacks on civilians, remains a pervasive and tragic element of the Israeli-Palestinian conflict. These acts are fueled not just by political grievances but by a deeply ingrained antisemitism that views Jews as an existential threat to the Palestinian cause. Whether through the targeting of civilians, the celebration of martyrdom, or the use of terror as a political tool, Palestinian groups have consistently employed violence to advance their agenda. This violence is inextricably linked to the broader cultural, religious, and ideological framework that defines the Palestinian rejection of Jewish legitimacy in the region. Until these deep-seated attitudes are addressed, it seems unlikely that the cycle of violence and hatred will ever cease.

Chapter 5: The Rejection of Peace Offers and the Unyielding Stance of Palestinian Leadership

The history of Israeli-Palestinian peace negotiations is marked by repeated rejection of peace offers by Palestinian leadership, despite numerous attempts by Israel and the international community to resolve the conflict. From the early days of the conflict to the present, Palestinian leaders have consistently rejected opportunities for peace, often with catastrophic consequences for both Israelis and Palestinians. This chapter will delve into these critical moments of rejection, highlighting the political, ideological, and strategic factors that have shaped Palestinian decisions.

The 1947 UN Partition Plan: The First Rejection

The roots of Palestinian rejectionism trace back to the earliest days of the Israeli state. In 1947, the United Nations proposed a partition plan to divide Palestine into two states: one Jewish and one Arab. The Jewish community accepted the plan, seeing it as a step toward establishing a national homeland after decades of persecution. However, Palestinian leaders, along with the surrounding Arab states, rejected the plan outright.

Yasser Arafat would later reflect on this early rejection:

> "In 1947, the Arabs rejected the UN Partition Plan because they believed that Palestine was an Arab land and that the Jews had no right to establish a state there."

This rejection set the tone for the Palestinian position in the decades that followed: the refusal to accept the legitimacy of a Jewish state in the Middle East, regardless of international agreements or the historical realities of Jewish presence in the land.

The 2000 Camp David Summit: A Missed Opportunity

The Camp David Summit in 2000 remains a pivotal moment in the history of Israeli-Palestinian peace negotiations, marked by unprecedented offers and devastating rejection. Israeli Prime Minister Ehud Barak, showing a willingness to make historic compromises, presented a plan that included the establishment of a Palestinian state in most of the West Bank and Gaza, with East Jerusalem as its capital. The proposal also addressed Palestinian concerns about refugees, offering mechanisms for compensation and a limited right of return. In return, Israel sought recognition as a Jewish state and guarantees for its security, including an end to claims and conflict.

President Bill Clinton, who mediated the talks, later recounted his frustration at the outcome: "Barak showed courage in taking risks for peace, offering more than anyone had ever offered before. But Arafat was either unwilling or unable to make the difficult decisions required for peace." Clinton emphasized that the failure was not due to the details of the plan but a lack of reciprocity from the Palestinian side.

Arafat's rejection and the subsequent outbreak of the Second Intifada shocked Israeli society. The wave of violence, which included suicide bombings and terror attacks targeting civilians, deepened Israeli skepticism about the possibility of peace. As Leslie Klaff notes, "The rejection of Camp David was not just a missed opportunity; it was a declaration that the Palestinian leadership prioritized the continuation of conflict over the establishment of a state."

Ehud Barak later reflected on the summit, stating: "We put everything on the table. We were ready to take enormous risks for peace, but Arafat refused to say yes. Instead, he chose violence. That moment revealed the true face of Palestinian rejectionism."

The Second Intifada, which followed the summit's collapse, left a devastating toll on both sides. More than 1,000 Israelis and thousands of Palestinians lost their lives, and the hopes for peace were replaced by heightened distrust and animosity. Tzipi Livni observed the long-term consequences: "The violence of the Intifada sent a clear message to Israelis—that even when we are willing to make painful concessions, we are met with rejection and terror."

The events at Camp David and their aftermath reinforced the perception that Palestinian rejectionism is not about borders or settlements but the very existence of Israel. As Gabriel Zaliasnik notes, "Arafat's actions at Camp David exposed the core issue: a refusal to acknowledge the Jewish people's right to self-determination in their historical homeland."

The rejection also had implications for Palestinian society. Instead of achieving statehood, Palestinians faced intensified Israeli security measures, a deteriorating economy, and a fractured political landscape. Tony Blair, reflecting on the broader impact, remarked: "Camp David was a turning point. It showed the world that peace cannot be achieved if one side is unwilling to recognize the other's basic rights."

The Global Impact of Rejection

The implications of the Camp David Summit extended far beyond Israel and Palestine. Ricardo Brodsky, an academic and public intellectual, emphasizes the broader significance of the summit's collapse: "Camp David demonstrated the complexity of the conflict: it's not merely about territorial disputes or the refugee issue, but about a refusal by the Palestinian leadership to recognize the legitimacy of the Jewish state. This rejection at Camp David deepened the cycle of violence, leading to further mistrust between the parties involved. We must understand this dynamic to prevent future failures in peace efforts."

Former UK Prime Minister Tony Blair highlighted the broader consequences: "The failure of Camp David was not just a tragedy for Israelis and Palestinians; it was a setback for the entire region. It underscored the need for a cultural and ideological shift in how the conflict is approached."

Leslie Klaff adds: "Camp David was a turning point that demonstrated how deeply ingrained Palestinian rejectionism is. The refusal to seize the opportunity for statehood was a disservice to their own people and a blow to global peace efforts."

Arafat's Role in the Collapse

The role of Yasser Arafat in the summit's failure remains a subject of intense scrutiny. Many leaders and analysts have pointed to his unwillingness to accept even the most generous offers as evidence of the Palestinian leadership's entrenched rejectionism. Bill Clinton noted in his memoirs: "Arafat could not bring himself to make the difficult decisions that would have led to peace. It became clear that his primary aim was not Palestinian statehood but rather the continuation of the conflict."

Sergio Micco, an expert in international relations, emphasizes that the rejection of peace was not merely a tactical decision but a sign of something more entrenched in Palestinian political culture: "The failure of Camp David in 2000 was a missed opportunity not just for Israel and Palestine, but for peace in the Middle East. Arafat's refusal to negotiate seriously with Barak and Clinton showed that the Palestinian leadership was more invested in perpetuating the conflict than in achieving a viable peace. This rejectionism, sadly, has become a defining characteristic of the Palestinian cause in many international arenas."

The Legacy of Rejectionism

The rejection of Camp David and its aftermath has had profound implications on both the Israeli-Palestinian conflict and global perceptions of the peace process. Ricardo Israel Zipper, a political analyst, argues: "The collapse of Camp David, especially Arafat's rejection, left a deep scar on the peace process. Israel made tremendous concessions, yet the outcome was a violent uprising. This moment showed that the core issue of the conflict is not just about land but about the fundamental recognition of Israel's right to exist as a Jewish state. Without that recognition, peace is impossible."

The consequences of the summit's failure continue to reverberate through Israeli and Palestinian societies. Ariela Agosin, a Chilean Jewish leader, reflects on the summit's aftermath: "Camp David revealed a painful truth—that peace requires two willing partners. Israel's willingness to compromise was met with rejection, and this rejection has echoed through subsequent decades of conflict."

The failure of the Camp David Summit ultimately reinforced the narrative that Palestinian rejectionism is not simply about territory, but a refusal to accept Israel's legitimacy as a Jewish state. The rejection led to decades of continued conflict, violence, and instability. As Ricardo Brodsky noted, "The rejection of Camp David set a precedent, signaling to the world that the Palestinian leadership was unwilling to engage in a constructive dialogue. This moment clarified the central challenge to peace—not the practical issues of territory, but the ideological denial of Israel's legitimacy."

Thus, the legacy of Camp David continues to shape the Israeli-Palestinian conflict, reminding the world of the profound obstacles to peace and the importance of recognizing both the practical and ideological dimensions of the conflict.

Bill Clinton, who brokered the Camp David Summit, remarked:

> "I thought Arafat was making a huge mistake. He had the opportunity to end the conflict. Israel offered more than anyone could have imagined, and yet, he chose violence instead."

For many analysts, the rejection of the Camp David offer was a pivotal moment that proved Palestinian leadership's unwillingness to compromise for peace. Michael Ehrlich, a Middle Eastern scholar at Bar Ilan University, has written:

> "Arafat's rejection of Camp David showed that Palestinian leadership was not interested in peace but in the destruction of Israel. It was a clear indication that peace would require a change in leadership."

This rejection not only resulted in the failure of the peace process but also set the stage for a new wave of violence, which set back the prospects for peace for years.

The 2008 Olmert Proposal: Another Rejection

In 2008, Ehud Olmert, then Israeli Prime Minister, presented another peace offer to Palestinian Authority President Mahmoud Abbas. This proposal included even more territorial concessions, including the establishment of a Palestinian state in nearly all of the West Bank, East Jerusalem as its capital, and a solution for the Gaza Strip. In exchange, Abbas would need to recognize Israel as a Jewish state and ensure the safety and security of Israel's citizens.

Once again, the Palestinian leadership rejected the offer. Abbas, like Arafat before him, insisted on further concessions, especially regarding the "right of return" for Palestinian refugees, a demand that would effectively undermine Israel's Jewish character.

Aviv Geffen, a political analyst and writer, reflected on the rejection:

> "The Palestinians had another chance to establish their own state, but they refused to compromise. At what point do we stop giving them chances and realize that they are not interested in peace?"

The rejection of this offer, similar to that of Camp David, revealed the deep unwillingness of Palestinian leadership to accept Israel's right to exist as a Jewish state. The repeated rejections of peace offers have left Israelis and the international community wondering whether Palestinian leadership is capable of accepting peace on any terms.

The Rise of Hamas and Its Impact on Peace Prospects

The rise of Hamas, an Islamist militant group, further complicated the situation. Founded in 1987 during the First Intifada, Hamas rejected the Oslo Accords, which were signed by the Palestine Liberation Organization (PLO) and Israel in the 1990s. The Oslo Accords provided a framework for peace, including mutual recognition between Israel and the PLO and the establishment of a Palestinian Authority. Hamas, however, refused to recognize Israel and called for its destruction, framing the conflict as a religious struggle rather than a political one.

Shimon Peres has pointed out the consequences of Hamas's stance:

> "Hamas has made it impossible for the Palestinians to negotiate peace with Israel. While Fatah might have been willing to compromise, Hamas has consistently chosen violence and terror over peace and coexistence."

Hamas's rejectionist stance became a key obstacle in the aftermath of the 2006 Palestinian legislative elections, which saw Hamas take control of Gaza. The group's refusal to recognize Israel, coupled with its violent tactics, ensured that any hopes for a two-state solution remained elusive. Hamas's control over Gaza has created a split between the Palestinian Authority in the West Bank and Hamas in Gaza, further complicating efforts for a unified Palestinian negotiating position.

Gabriel Zaliasnik, an expert on Middle Eastern politics, argues:

> "The rise of Hamas and its hardline rejection of any form of coexistence with Israel has effectively killed any prospect for peace. The Palestinian leadership must choose between peace and extremism, but so far, they have chosen extremism."

The International Community's Role in Palestinian Rejectionism

The international community, including the United Nations and major global powers, has played a mixed role in the Israeli-Palestinian conflict. While many Western governments have pressured Israel to make concessions, the same level of pressure has not been applied to Palestinian leadership, particularly regarding their rejection of peace offers.

Ricardo Brodsky, a political analyst, notes:

> "There is a double standard in how the international community treats the conflict. Palestinian rejectionism is rarely addressed, and the leadership continues to be coddled, despite their refusal to negotiate peace."

International organizations, such as UNRWA (United Nations Relief and Works Agency), which provides assistance to Palestinian refugees, have often failed to hold Palestinian leaders accountable for rejecting peace offers. Instead, they have perpetuated a narrative that excuses Palestinian rejectionism while placing blame solely on Israel.

Claudio Grossman, a noted international law expert, has criticized the lack of accountability:

> "The international community must stop excusing Palestinian rejectionism and start holding both sides to the same standard. Until there is an honest reckoning with the facts, peace will remain an unattainable dream."

The Path Forward: A Shift in Leadership and Mindset

For real peace to be achieved, Palestinian leadership must be willing to abandon its rejectionist policies and embrace a new approach. This requires not only a shift in political strategy but also a change in the cultural mindset that has dominated Palestinian society for decades. Pilar Rahola, a Spanish journalist and political commentator, argues:

> "The rejection of peace is not a sustainable strategy. Eventually, the Palestinian leadership will have to accept the reality of Israel's existence and engage in meaningful negotiations."

The future of peace in the region will depend on whether Palestinian leaders are willing to accept Israel as a legitimate partner for peace, whether the Palestinian people demand a change in leadership, and whether the international community can foster a more balanced and honest dialogue.

The consistent rejection of peace by Palestinian leadership is a defining feature of the Israeli-Palestinian conflict. From the UN Partition Plan of 1947 to the Camp David Summit and the Olmert proposal, Palestinian leadership has repeatedly walked away from opportunities to resolve the conflict. This rejection has been fueled by a combination of nationalism, religious ideology, and political calculations. Until the Palestinian leadership is willing to accept Israel's right to exist and engage in meaningful peace negotiations, the prospect of a lasting resolution

The Global Denunciation of UNRWA and the Palestinian Narrative

As the international community grapples with the resurgence of antisemitism and the complexities of the Israeli-Palestinian conflict, one of the key institutions that has been central to the Palestinian cause is the United Nations Relief and Works Agency (UNRWA). Initially set up to provide humanitarian aid to Palestinian refugees displaced after the 1948 Arab-Israeli War, UNRWA has been at the center of significant controversy for its role in perpetuating a narrative that many critics argue is detrimental to peace and reconciliation between Israel and the Palestinians.

UNRWA was created to address the immediate humanitarian crisis caused by the displacement of Palestinians following the Arab-Israeli War in 1948, and its mission was primarily focused on delivering basic services such as healthcare, education, and housing to Palestinian refugees in camps throughout the region. However, over time, its mandate and its activities evolved into something far more political, with its influence and legacy becoming a critical focal point in the ongoing debate about the Israeli-Palestinian conflict.

The Right of Return: A Central, Contentious Issue

The most controversial aspect of UNRWA's role in the conflict lies in its emphasis on the "right of return" for Palestinian refugees. This right, enshrined in the United Nations General Assembly Resolution 194 passed in 1948, has been interpreted by Palestinians as the entitlement for not only those who were displaced during the 1948 war but also their descendants, to return to the land that was lost during the creation of Israel. As of today, millions of people in the Palestinian diaspora claim this right, which, according to many observers, represents a direct challenge to the notion of Israel as a Jewish state.

Critics of UNRWA, including scholars like Michael Ehrlich and Gabriel Zaliasnik, have argued that the continued· emphasis on the right of return has not only contributed to the perpetuation of Palestinian refugee status across multiple generations but also actively undermines the prospects for peace in the region. Rather than encouraging the integration of Palestinian refugees into their host countries or helping them move forward with their lives, UNRWA has entrenched the idea that the only resolution to the Palestinian refugee issue is the return of all refugees to their former homes within what is now the State of Israel. This demand, which is often framed as a fundamental and inalienable right, has been one of the major sticking points in Israeli-Palestinian negotiations, with Israel categorically rejecting it as a non-negotiable condition for peace.

From Israel's perspective, the right of return is not just a humanitarian concern; it is a strategic and existential one. Accepting the return of millions of Palestinians would alter the demographic balance of Israel, endangering the Jewish character of the state. For Israelis, the demand is seen not just as a call for justice, but as a political and existential challenge that seeks to negate the very foundation of Israel as a sovereign Jewish state. Therefore, the insistence on the right of return becomes not only a humanitarian issue but a political flashpoint that prevents a more balanced and realistic peace process.

Perpetuation of Refugee Status: A Cycle of Dependency and Resentment

By continually emphasizing the right of return, UNRWA has been accused of maintaining a state of perpetual victimhood and dependency among Palestinian refugees. While the humanitarian needs of these refugees are undeniable, the focus on return rather than integration has meant that for generations, Palestinian refugees have remained in a liminal state, with little hope of either returning to their homeland or integrating into their host countries. This situation has created a cycle in which refugees are sustained by international aid, but without any clear pathway to a stable future. The refugee camps, rather than being temporary shelters for those displaced by war, have become permanent homes for millions of people living in difficult and often impoverished conditions.

UNRWA has become a central institution in this cycle of dependency, providing services such as education, healthcare, and food aid to millions of refugees. While these services are undoubtedly necessary, critics argue that they have contributed to a mentality of reliance rather than self-sufficiency. UNRWA's status as the primary provider of humanitarian aid to Palestinians has entrenched the idea that the only resolution to the refugee issue is the return to Israel, thus preventing refugees from moving forward with their lives or finding new opportunities for stability and prosperity.

For many Palestinians, especially younger generations who have never lived in Israel, the idea of return is more symbolic than practical. Yet, UNRWA's continued focus on return as a central theme in its educational materials and messaging reinforces the notion that the refugee issue is not only unresolved but that it can only be solved by the ultimate return of Palestinians to their ancestral homes. This has created a situation in which many refugees hold onto the belief that peace is only achievable if their right to return is fully recognized, a stance that directly conflicts with Israel's position on the matter and stymies meaningful negotiations toward a lasting peace agreement.

UNRWA's Influence on Palestinian Identity and Political Aspirations

Beyond its humanitarian role, UNRWA's actions have also played a pivotal role in shaping Palestinian identity and political aspirations. By continuously promoting the idea that the Palestinian refugee problem is not only a humanitarian issue but also a political one, UNRWA has become an institution that helps define Palestinian nationalism. The refugee narrative, tied closely to the right of return, has become central to Palestinian identity, framing the conflict in terms of displacement, justice, and historical wrongs that need to be rectified.

For Palestinians, especially in refugee camps, the right of return is not just a political demand—it is a deeply ingrained part of their collective memory and cultural identity. This narrative has been passed down through generations, reinforcing the idea that their connection to the land is unbroken and that the return to their ancestral homes is both a moral and legal imperative. In this way, UNRWA has contributed to the formation of a narrative that sustains Palestinian identity while simultaneously complicating efforts to move past the historical trauma of 1948.

While this narrative has provided a sense of purpose and unity for many Palestinians, it has also contributed to the perpetuation of a conflict that refuses to move beyond the past. The focus on return and the perpetuation of refugee status have overshadowed efforts to build a future based on mutual recognition, peaceful coexistence, and reconciliation. As a result, UNRWA's stance on the right of return has often been seen as a hindrance to the creation of a more forward-looking Palestinian identity that focuses on coexistence and peaceful coexistence alongside Israel.

UNRWA's Political Bias and Neutrality Concerns

Another significant issue that has come under scrutiny in recent years is UNRWA's alleged political bias. While UNRWA's mandate is ostensibly humanitarian, the agency has often been accused of taking sides in the Israeli-Palestinian conflict. Critics have pointed to instances in which UNRWA employees have expressed anti-Israel views or supported groups considered by Israel and the international community to be terrorist organizations, such as Hamas.

In some cases, it has been reported that UNRWA staff have openly praised groups like Hamas, whose ideology calls for the destruction of Israel, or have posted anti-Israel content on social media. These actions have raised concerns about the agency's neutrality and its ability to serve as an impartial actor in the conflict. If UNRWA is seen as aligning itself with one side of the conflict, it risks undermining its credibility and effectiveness in promoting peace, reconciliation, and humanitarian relief. This is particularly problematic given that UNRWA receives significant funding from Western nations, including the United States and European Union, who have both criticized the agency's perceived bias and its failure to remain neutral in its operations.

The Role of UNRWA in Regional Stability

The Palestinian refugee issue has regional implications that extend beyond Israel and the Palestinian territories. Palestinian refugees reside in significant numbers in neighboring Arab countries, particularly Jordan, Lebanon, and Syria. In Jordan, Palestinian refugees make up a substantial portion of the population, and while many have been granted citizenship, the issue of their status remains sensitive. In

Lebanon, Palestinian refugees live in crowded and impoverished camps and face significant social and legal discrimination, while in Syria, the refugee population has been deeply affected by the ongoing civil war.

The presence of large Palestinian refugee populations in these countries has created social and political tensions, contributing to instability in the region. The lack of resolution to the refugee issue, perpetuated by UNRWA's focus on return, has meant that Palestinian refugees remain a source of political leverage for various factions and states in the region. This has made it difficult to address the issue of Palestinian refugees in a way that ensures their integration into their host countries or provides them with long-term solutions.

Moving Toward a New Framework

As the political landscape evolves, it is becoming increasingly clear that UNRWA's current approach is not conducive to long-term peace. While the agency has played a vital role in providing humanitarian assistance to Palestinian refugees, its continued focus on the right of return, as well as its perceived political bias, has hindered progress toward a peaceful resolution of the conflict. The international community must reconsider the role of UNRWA in the context of the changing dynamics of the Israeli-Palestinian conflict.

A new approach to Palestinian refugee assistance must prioritize integration, resettlement, and development rather than the perpetuation of a status quo rooted in historical grievances. This could involve creating new frameworks for addressing the needs of refugees in a manner that promotes stability, security, and coexistence. Only by embracing a more pragmatic and forward-thinking approach to the refugee issue can the international community hope to create the conditions for lasting peace in the region.

The role of UNRWA in the Israeli-Palestinian conflict, particularly its promotion of the right of return and its involvement in shaping

Palestinian identity and political aspirations, has been a central factor in the ongoing intractability of the conflict. While UNR

Gabriel Zaliasnik has stated:

"The perpetuation of the refugee issue by UNRWA is not an act of charity, it is a political act designed to undermine Israel's legitimacy. The fact that the agency has been allowed to perpetuate this myth for decades shows a failure of the international community to demand accountability."

Furthermore, critics of UNRWA argue that its policies contribute to a culture of victimhood, rather than one of self-reliance or progress. By focusing on the perpetuation of Palestinian victimhood rather than encouraging integration or self-sufficiency, UNRWA inadvertently hinders any long-term prospects for peace. Renowned philosopher and public intellectual Bernard-Henri Lévy also weighed in on this issue, remarking:

> "By continuing to portray the Palestinians as eternal victims, UNRWA helps reinforce a narrative that keeps them stuck in the past. This agency is not leading Palestinians towards a better future—it is keeping them in a state of perpetual grievance." (Lévy, 2023)

Lévy's criticism speaks to a broader concern: that UNRWA's actions, by continually focusing on the past and nurturing a sense of unfulfilled entitlement, prevent Palestinian society from moving forward and finding pathways to peace. The narrative of victimhood, while validating the experiences of Palestinian refugees, also limits their future prospects and entrenches the conflict further.

Another significant point of contention is the role UNRWA plays in fostering the belief that Palestinian refugees, including generations born after the original 1948 exodus, have an intrinsic right to return to their ancestral homes within Israel. The right of return has been a major sticking point in peace negotiations, as Israel has consistently argued that such a return would undermine the Jewish character of the state. The insistence on the right of return by UNRWA has thus been viewed as a key obstacle to achieving a two-state solution.

David Ben Gurion, Israel's first Prime Minister, clearly articulated Israel's stance on the right of return, asserting:

> "The Arab refugees who left will not return. There can be no peace with the Palestinians until they accept that there is no return to 1948."

Ben Gurion's words reflect Israel's foundational belief that the return of Palestinian refugees to Israel proper is incompatible with the existence of a Jewish state. This position has not only been pivotal in Israel's security policies but also central to the peace process.

Critics, including analysts like Michael Ehrlich, emphasize that the lack of any meaningful initiative by UNRWA to resettle refugees in their host countries or to promote integration has left millions of Palestinians in a perpetual state of dependency. They argue that UNRWA's operations create a narrative of a future return to a pre-1948 reality, rather than focusing on the realistic and achievable goal of creating a Palestinian state.

"UNRWA's refusal to adapt to changing realities only exacerbates the plight of refugees and keeps Palestinians trapped in an endless cycle of frustration," Ehrlich remarked. "The agency's unwillingness to recognize the legitimacy of Israel and its role in the region serves no one's interests."

This approach has fueled not only political tension but also humanitarian stagnation. While international aid is essential for addressing the immediate needs of refugees, critics argue that UNRWA's focus on the "right of return" rather than resettlement has hampered the long-term development of Palestinian refugees, contributing to their ongoing struggles and preventing the resolution of the refugee issue in a sustainable manner.

The international community's failure to hold UNRWA accountable for its continued perpetuation of the Palestinian narrative has led to growing criticism from multiple fronts. Many argue that without a shift in this approach, the prospects for any lasting peace will remain bleak.

Aviv Geffen, a noted political commentator and Israeli analyst, has highlighted how the narrative perpetuated by UNRWA plays into the broader rejectionist attitudes within Palestinian leadership:

> "The persistence of the 'right of return' idea is a deliberate obstruction to any peace process. As long as Palestinian leadership continues to cling to this, there can be no meaningful dialogue or peace. UNRWA's stance simply mirrors the rejectionist policies that dominate Palestinian politics."

Israeli Arab leaders, who often face a complex balancing act between their Arab heritage and their Israeli citizenship, also see the negative impact of UNRWA's policies. Arab-Israeli legislator Ayman Odeh expressed:

> "The Palestinian refugee issue cannot be solved by perpetuating a vision of return to lands within Israel. The focus should be on building a future where Palestinians and Israelis live side by side, with mutual respect and understanding, not on resurrecting past grievances."

This perspective underscores the reality that the refugee issue, as currently framed by organizations like UNRWA, exacerbates existing divisions, preventing Arabs and Jews from moving beyond historical narratives to pursue reconciliation and peace.

On the other hand, pro-Israel voices argue that the international community's silence on UNRWA's policies further complicates the situation. Miri Regev, Israel's Minister of Transportation and a vocal proponent of Israel's right to defend itself, commented:

> "The world needs to realize that by financing and supporting organizations like UNRWA, they are empowering a narrative of hate and rejection. These institutions should not be allowed to dictate the terms of peace. Israel's right to exist and its security cannot be compromised by historical revisionism."

Pro-Israel activists have long pointed out that the international community's tendency to turn a blind eye to Palestinian rejectionism, whether through UNRWA's perpetuation of refugee status or through widespread support for the 'right of return,' creates an imbalance in the peace process. According to former U.S. Ambassador to the United Nations, Nikki Haley:

> "The U.S. will not support an institution that fosters the perpetuation of a narrative that demonizes Israel, rejects its right to exist, and fuels extremism. UNRWA needs to be held accountable for its role in perpetuating the conflict."

Gabriel Zaliasnik, an influential Jewish leader from Chile, has also weighed in on the dangers of continuing this narrative, stating:

"UNRWA is not just an aid agency; it has become a political instrument that nurtures an illusion of a return to a bygone era, one that is incompatible with the realities of the modern Middle East."

As the world continues to seek a peaceful resolution to the Israeli-Palestinian conflict, the role of UNRWA cannot be overlooked.

The agency's policies, particularly its stance on the right of return and its perpetuation of a narrative of victimhood, have served to perpetuate the conflict and stall meaningful dialogue. To move towards peace, a shift is necessary, both in the approach of UNRWA and in the broader Palestinian narrative—one that embraces the possibilities of integration, self-determination, and coexistence, rather than the endless pursuit of historical grievances.

The global denunciation of UNRWA and its role in maintaining the Palestinian narrative presents a challenge to the peace process. By perpetuating the refugee issue and reinforcing a culture of victimhood, the agency has contributed to the entrenchment of the conflict. For peace to be achievable, a new narrative must emerge—one that encourages coexistence, integration, and mutual recognition between Israelis and Palestinians. This will require not only a rethinking of UNRWA's mission but also a broader shift in how the international community addresses the issues that have plagued this conflict for over seven decades.

Chapter 6

Jaime Quintana: A Voice for Pragmatic Human Rights Advocacy

Jaime Quintana, a Chilean senator and long-time advocate for human rights, has consistently critiqued foreign policies that focus on symbolic gestures rather than substantial solutions to global issues.

Feeling Well: Quintana argues that many foreign policy actions are motivated more by public sentiment or moral alignment than by actual impacts on the ground. For instance, symbolic resolutions that endorse the Palestinian cause, while often politically popular, can be seen as hollow when they fail to bring about practical change in the lives of Palestinians or Israelis. These actions are a way of "feeling good" about taking a stance without addressing deeper geopolitical complexities.

Doing Well: Quintana emphasizes the importance of focusing on concrete, tangible initiatives that foster meaningful dialogue and cooperation. He advocates for practical solutions such as cross-border economic ventures, joint educational projects, and infrastructure development as ways to create long-term peace. Quintana's perspective suggests that "doing well" involves engaging in actions that create conditions for mutual prosperity and lasting coexistence, rather than simply making statements that do little to address the core issues.

Pedro Araya: Regional Diplomacy and Practical Solutions

Pedro Araya, a Chilean senator with deep ties to international diplomacy, often speaks about Chile's role in shaping pragmatic and results-driven foreign policies.

Feeling Well: Araya acknowledges that symbolic foreign policy decisions, such as voicing support for one side of the Israeli-Palestinian conflict, are often driven by public opinion or ideological considerations. These gestures might satisfy the emotional need for moral clarity but frequently fail to provide solutions to the underlying problems. For example, voting in favor of UN resolutions that criticize Israel without also addressing the Palestinian leadership's role in perpetuating conflict might make people feel like they've done something important, but it does little to help resolve the conflict itself.

Doing Well: Araya stresses that Chile should align its foreign policy with actions that have measurable, positive impacts on the ground. His advocacy for economic partnerships, educational exchanges, and collaborative infrastructure projects highlights a practical approach to international relations that values results over rhetoric. For Araya, "doing well" means addressing the root causes of conflict through tangible measures that bring people together and promote sustainable solutions, rather than simply seeking moral victories that are more about optics than effectiveness.

Marco Núñez, former president of the Chilean Chamber of Deputies, has a background in human rights and social justice, with a focus on how international diplomacy and aid intersect with grassroots development.

Feeling Well: Núñez critiques the international tendency to make grand statements about human rights or offer aid without asking whether these efforts truly change the lives of people in need. The "feeling well" approach often manifests in the form of symbolic actions, like public condemnations of human rights violations or humanitarian assistance that does not tackle the structural issues causing these violations. For Núñez, these actions may look good on paper but rarely lead to sustainable peace or improvements in the quality of life for marginalized communities.

Doing Well: Núñez advocates for a "doing well" approach that focuses on empowering communities through long-term social programs. His support for education, healthcare, and economic opportunity as central tenets of foreign aid is a call to address the root causes of poverty and conflict. He believes that true social justice cannot be achieved through gestures alone but requires a comprehensive, grassroots approach that gives people the tools to overcome adversity and build peaceful, prosperous societies.

—-

José Miguel Insulza: Diplomatic Leadership and Accountability

José Miguel Insulza, a former Chilean politician and former Secretary-General of the Organization of American States (OAS), is a seasoned diplomat who has witnessed the limitations of symbolic international actions.

Feeling Well: Insulza has often spoken about the limitations of international aid programs that focus on symbolic gestures, such as voting in favor of UN resolutions that condemn one side of a conflict, without considering the long-term consequences. He sees such actions as satisfying immediate moral inclinations but insufficient in addressing the real issues that cause conflict and suffering. For example, some aid programs fail to address the need for self-reliance and economic independence among Palestinian refugees, often perpetuating cycles of dependence rather than fostering empowerment.

Doing Well: Insulza advocates for reforming international organizations like the United Nations Relief and Works Agency (UNRWA) to ensure that aid addresses the root causes of issues like refugee status and poverty. He emphasizes the importance of multilateral diplomacy and accountability, arguing that international efforts must be focused on creating self-sustaining solutions that empower local populations. "Doing well," for Insulza, involves using diplomatic tools to address the structural inequalities that fuel conflict, such as poverty, lack of education, and political instability.

—-

Luis Almagro: The Current OAS Perspective

Luis Almagro, the Secretary-General of the Organization of American States (OAS), has been vocal about the role of international organizations in addressing human rights and democracy.

Feeling Well: Almagro has criticized the way international aid is often delivered through performative acts, such as one-sided resolutions or condemnation of certain governments or actors, that appeal to popular sentiment but do little to create real change. He sees this approach as morally satisfying but ineffectual in promoting democratic principles and human rights.

Doing Well: Almagro advocates for a more nuanced and results-oriented approach to foreign policy, emphasizing initiatives that focus on building democratic institutions, fostering economic independence, and promoting human rights in a tangible way. His support for multilateral efforts that empower local populations through education, democratic governance, and economic development embodies a "doing well" approach, where sustainable solutions are prioritized over symbolic actions.

—-

Ricardo Lagos Escobar: Statesmanship and Long-Term Vision

Ricardo Lagos Escobar, former president of Chile, is known for his long-term vision and commitment to multilateral diplomacy.

Feeling Well: Lagos has often critiqued the tendency of the international community to focus on symbolic actions, like humanitarian aid or public condemnation of specific regimes, without addressing the structural issues that underlie global conflicts. These gestures, while morally fulfilling, often fail to bring about lasting change.

Doing Well: Lagos emphasizes the need for comprehensive, long-term investments in infrastructure, education, and economic development to create self-sustaining communities. His belief in regional cooperation and multilateralism as the keys to solving conflicts aligns with a "doing well" philosophy, where concrete actions are taken to address the root causes of issues such as poverty, inequality, and political instability.

—-

Eduardo Frei Ruiz-Tagle: Pragmatic Development Advocacy

Eduardo Frei Ruiz-Tagle, another former Chilean president, has long been an advocate for pragmatic and sustainable foreign policy solutions.

Feeling Well: Frei has expressed concerns about international aid policies that focus more on creating a positive image for donor countries rather than addressing the long-term needs of recipient communities. While these policies may make the international community "feel good" about their contributions, they often fail to solve the deeper structural issues at play.

Doing Well: Frei's approach advocates for policies that create lasting change, focusing on education, economic development, and regional cooperation. He supports development programs that are aligned with measurable outcomes, ensuring that foreign aid contributes to self-reliance and fosters long-term stability.

—-

Juan Gabriel Valdés: Diplomacy and Constructive Engagement

Juan Gabriel Valdés, former Chilean Foreign Minister and a seasoned diplomat, has a clear vision of how multilateral diplomacy can achieve real results.

Feeling Well: Valdés critiques the use of foreign policy as a tool for scoring moral victories through symbolic actions. He argues that such measures, like endorsing one side of a conflict without understanding the complexity of the situation, may serve to assuage public opinion but fail to address the root causes of the conflict.

Doing Well: Valdés advocates for pragmatic, results-oriented diplomacy that seeks to foster dialogue and collaboration, particularly through multilateral frameworks. He stresses the importance of addressing the root causes of conflict through economic, educational, and diplomatic efforts that empower local communities and create lasting peace.

—-

Guido Girardi: Health, Rights, and Global Diplomacy

Guido Girardi, a Chilean senator and advocate for public health, often brings a perspective that integrates humanitarian concerns with pragmatic solutions.

Feeling Well: Girardi is critical of international efforts that prioritize moral high ground over meaningful solutions. He sees symbolic gestures, like condemning human rights abuses or sending humanitarian aid without follow-up, as acts that often do not result in substantial improvements.

Doing Well: Girardi advocates for policies that not only address immediate needs but also focus on long-term solutions like public health infrastructure, education, and economic development. His approach suggests that true humanitarian work involves empowering communities to overcome challenges independently, rather than perpetuating cycles of dependency.

—-

Conclusion: Latin American Perspectives on Diplomacy and Human Rights

The collective insights of figures like Jaime Quintana, Pedro Araya, Marco Núñez, José Miguel Insulza, Luis Almagro, Ricardo Lagos Escobar, Eduardo Frei Ruiz-Tagle, Juan Gabriel Valdés, Ricardo Brodsky, Miguel Steuermann, and Guido Girardi offer a nuanced and multifaceted

Chapter 7

6. The Distortion of History: Holocaust Inversion as a Political Tool

Holocaust inversion, a rhetorical strategy where the roles of the victims and perpetrators of the Holocaust are reversed, is a particularly insidious form of historical distortion. This tactic has been increasingly used to portray Israel as engaging in actions akin to the Nazi regime's genocidal policies during World War II. This comparison is not only misleading but serves a dual purpose: it delegitimizes the State of Israel while simultaneously weaponizing the trauma of the Holocaust for political ends.

Andres Tassara, an Israeli scholar specializing in international relations, has spoken at length about the dangers of Holocaust inversion, which he views as a politically motivated form of historical manipulation. Tassara warns that invoking Holocaust language to describe Israel's military actions in Gaza or the West Bank misrepresents the intentions and actions of the Israeli government, and, in doing so, undermines the significance of the Holocaust itself. He explains that while Israel's actions may be seen by some as disproportionate or heavy-handed, they are fundamentally defensive in nature, aimed at protecting the country from threats posed by terrorist organizations such as Hamas.

By contrast, the Nazi regime's actions were systematic, ideologically driven, and genocidal, aiming to exterminate entire populations based on race and ethnicity. Farcas draws a stark line between these two scenarios, noting that any attempt to equate Israel's military strategy with the Holocaust not only distorts historical facts but also trivializes the suffering of six million Jews who perished under Nazi rule.

This pattern of Holocaust inversion is not a new phenomenon, but it has gained traction in contemporary political discourse, particularly in the Middle East and parts of Europe. Political leaders, intellectuals, and activists have used Holocaust analogies to condemn Israel's military operations, with the term "genocide" frequently thrown around without basis in fact. This is exemplified in the discourse surrounding the Gaza conflict, where Israel's military operations, aimed at neutralizing Hamas fighters and military infrastructure, are framed as part of a broader campaign to eradicate Palestinians as a people. This rhetoric, according to Farcas, not only misrepresents the nature of the conflict but also leads to the erasure of the unique horror of the Holocaust itself.

Farcas notes, "Using Holocaust rhetoric to describe the situation in Gaza is not just a simplification of a complex political situation—it is a deliberate distortion that undermines the memory of the Holocaust and its moral significance." He argues that this false equivalence between Israeli defensive measures and Nazi genocide is not just a historical inaccuracy but also a dangerous tactic that feeds into the global narrative of anti-Israel sentiment, which often crosses into antisemitism. As historian Lesley Klaff highlights, the use of Holocaust analogies in this context is not only misleading but also deeply offensive to the memory of the millions who suffered and died in the Holocaust.

7. The Global Spread of Holocaust Inversion

Holocaust inversion has transcended national borders, particularly in the context of the Israeli-Palestinian conflict. The strategy has gained significant traction in both the Middle East and Europe, where political groups and public figures increasingly adopt Holocaust language to criticize Israeli policies. For example, during the Gaza conflict of 2008-2009, the rhetoric of "Israeli genocide" and "Israeli occupation" gained considerable momentum, with many comparing Israel's military actions to Nazi atrocities. This narrative has only intensified in recent years, especially with the rise of populist movements in Europe and the Middle East.

The spread of Holocaust inversion has been particularly pronounced in the Arab world, where it has become a central feature of anti-Israel rhetoric. Palestinian leaders, along with various Arab political figures, often employ Holocaust language to describe Israeli military actions, referring to them as "genocidal" or equating them to Nazi crimes. This tactic not only simplifies the complexities of the Israeli-Palestinian conflict but also shifts the moral conversation, redirecting blame away from Palestinian leadership and focusing it instead on Israel.

Farcas underscores the dangers of this rhetoric, noting, "By invoking the Holocaust in relation to Israel, you not only dishonor the memory of its victims but also distort the real issues at the heart of the Palestinian-Israeli conflict." The use of Holocaust imagery in this way works to reinforce a victim narrative that absolves Palestinian leadership of responsibility for the ongoing violence and political dysfunction within Palestinian territories. Furthermore, it enables the manipulation of global sentiment by painting Israel as the sole aggressor, thus erasing the context of Hamas's role in perpetuating the violence.

This inversion of history also plays a central role in the rising tide of antisemitism in Europe and elsewhere. As scholars like Michael Ehrlich and Lesley Klaff point out, when Holocaust comparisons are used to vilify Israel, it becomes more difficult for the international community to differentiate between legitimate criticism of Israeli policy and the demonization of Jews as a whole. Klaff warns, "By using the Holocaust as a political weapon, these movements risk delegitimizing the very moral lessons we are meant to draw from the Holocaust—lessons that teach us to fight hatred and intolerance in all their forms."

8. The Moral and Political Implications of Holocaust Inversion

The consequences of Holocaust inversion are far-reaching, both politically and morally. Politically, it undermines the legitimacy of Israel's right to defend itself, casting Israel as a colonial power or an oppressor in a conflict that is fundamentally about security. This narrative, repeated often enough, creates a distorted view of the Middle East conflict, one that neglects the terrorist threats that Israel faces from groups like Hamas, Hezbollah, and other jihadist organizations.

Morally, Holocaust inversion creates a dangerous parallel to Holocaust denial. Just as Holocaust denial seeks to erase or distort the historical reality of Nazi atrocities, Holocaust inversion works to erase the unique lessons that the Holocaust provides about intolerance, racism, and genocide. It diminishes the horrific experiences of the millions who suffered and died in the Holocaust by applying the term "genocide" to a situation that does not meet the criteria of systematic extermination.

Farcas emphasizes the importance of preserving the moral integrity of the Holocaust memory, warning, "The use of Holocaust language in this context not only distorts history—it actively harms the fight against contemporary forms of hatred and prejudice." Farcas, like many others, calls for a return to truth in discourse. By focusing on the real, complex issues that drive the Israeli-Palestinian conflict—namely, the security needs of Israel and the political divisions among Palestinian leadership—the global community can move away from oversimplified narratives that do more harm than good.

Chapter 9. Confronting Holocaust Inversion: The Path Forward

Confronting Holocaust inversion requires a collective effort from educators, scholars, politicians, and civil society. The first step is to engage with history honestly and transparently, recognizing the unique historical tragedy of the Holocaust while also addressing contemporary issues with clarity. As Bernard-Henri Lévy and Michael Ehrlich argue, it is essential to educate future generations about the Holocaust not just as an isolated historical event but as a moral imperative to prevent such horrors from happening again. This education must also include a critical understanding of how historical events are used and misused in contemporary political discourse.

Farcas calls for more rigorous Holocaust education to prevent the distortion of its lessons. "If we allow the Holocaust to be hijacked by political movements for ideological purposes, we risk losing not only the memory of the victims but also the moral guidance the Holocaust offers for confronting intolerance and hatred in the present." He stresses that we must educate both the general public and political leaders about the dangers of Holocaust inversion and its role in fostering antisemitism and political extremism.

This fight against Holocaust inversion is not only about protecting historical truth but also about safeguarding the future. If we allow the moral lessons of the Holocaust to be obscured by political agendas, we risk repeating the very patterns of hatred and violence that led to that dark chapter in human history. As Daniel Farcas concludes, "The struggle against Holocaust inversion is not just about defending Israel—it is about defending the very principles of truth, justice, and human dignity."

This expanded chapter integrates deeper analysis, drawing from the insights of Daniel Farcas and other scholars like Michael Ehrlich, while providing further context on the global spread and moral dangers of Holocaust inversion.

Chapter 10: The Global Denunciation of UNRWA and the Palestinian Narrative

As the world witnesses a rise in antisemitism, alongside the perpetuation of the Israeli-Palestinian conflict, one institution that has been a key player in shaping the Palestinian narrative is the United Nations Relief and Works Agency (UNRWA). Established in 1949, UNRWA was originally intended as a temporary humanitarian relief body, tasked with providing essential services and aid to Palestinian refugees displaced by the 1948 Arab-Israeli War. The conflict, which resulted in the establishment of the State of Israel, caused the mass displacement of hundreds of thousands of Palestinians who fled or were expelled from their homes. UNRWA's mandate was to provide aid, including food, shelter, and education, to these refugees, many of whom found themselves in neighboring countries such as Jordan, Lebanon, and Syria, or in territories such as the West Bank and Gaza Strip, then under Arab control.

However, what was meant to be a short-term emergency response has, over seven decades, transformed into a deeply entrenched and politically charged organization that has become synonymous with the Palestinian refugee issue. Instead of resolving the crisis of Palestinian refugees, critics argue that UNRWA has, over time, exacerbated it, playing an active role in preserving the refugee status of millions of Palestinians across multiple generations. In doing so, the agency has inadvertently contributed to a political narrative that has hindered peace and reconciliation between Israelis and Palestinians.

The core issue lies in UNRWA's continued recognition of the descendants of the original 1948 refugees as refugees themselves. Unlike other refugee populations around the world, where refugee status typically ends after one generation, UNRWA has kept this status alive through successive generations. This means that the children, grandchildren, and even great-grandchildren of Palestinians displaced in 1948 are still classified as refugees. This policy has created a refugee identity that stretches across multiple generations, one that has become central to Palestinian identity.

By perpetuating the refugee status of these individuals, UNRWA has, according to many critics, turned what was intended to be a humanitarian initiative into a politically charged issue. Critics such as Michael Ehrlich and Gabriel Zaliasnik argue that the agency's actions have not only prolonged the refugee crisis but have also deepened the entrenched political narratives that make peace negotiations increasingly difficult. For Palestinians, the refugee issue, and particularly the right of return, has become a central aspect of their identity and a demand that is consistently emphasized by Palestinian leadership. The "right of return" refers to the demand that Palestinian refugees, as well as their descendants, be allowed to return to the land they fled in 1948, now part of the State of Israel. This demand has been a major point of contention in peace talks and is often viewed by Israeli leaders as a nonstarter, as the return of millions of Palestinians would alter the demographic makeup of Israel and undermine its identity as a Jewish state.

Gabriel Zaliasnik, a prominent Chilean political analyst, has been one of the harshest critics of UNRWA's approach. He argues that: "The perpetuation of the refugee issue by UNRWA is not an act of charity; it is a political act designed to undermine Israel's legitimacy. The fact that the agency has been allowed to perpetuate this myth for decades shows a failure of the international community to demand accountability."

Zaliasnik's perspective highlights the political nature of UNRWA's actions. By continuously emphasizing the "right of return," UNRWA has, in his view, actively contributed to the delegitimization of Israel, rather than helping to resolve the underlying issues that sustain the conflict. The refugee status has become a symbol of Palestinian dispossession and has been used to rally international support against

Israel, making any efforts toward peace and compromise seem futile. The international community's failure to hold UNRWA accountable for perpetuating this stance has, according to Zaliasnik, helped to perpetuate the cycle of conflict, making it harder for both sides to reconcile their differences.

Critics also argue that the continuation of the refugee issue has led to the creation of a "culture of victimhood" among Palestinians. Instead of fostering self-reliance, economic independence, and a future-oriented outlook, UNRWA's approach has, some say, entrenched a mindset of perpetual grievance. Bernard-Henri Lévy, a French philosopher and public intellectual, has weighed in on this aspect of the debate, suggesting that: "By continuing to portray the Palestinians as eternal victims, UNRWA helps reinforce a narrative that keeps them stuck in the past. This agency is not leading Palestinians towards a better future—it is keeping them in a state of perpetual grievance."

Lévy's criticism of UNRWA is rooted in the idea that the agency's focus on the refugee status, the right of return, and the perpetuation of victimhood has prevented Palestinians from moving forward. Rather than empowering Palestinians to build a better future, he argues, the narrative reinforced by UNRWA keeps them trapped in the past, fixated on historical grievances. This, in turn, has hindered efforts to develop a forward-looking peace process based on mutual respect and compromise. The ongoing portrayal of Palestinians as victims, without a shift toward self-determination and self-reliance, has contributed to a sense of hopelessness that further entrenches the conflict.

UNRWA's continued existence and its policies have also faced significant criticism within the international community. Several Western countries, including the United States, have expressed their dissatisfaction with the agency's approach, particularly its insistence on the "right of return." The United States, under the Trump administration, even cut funding to UNRWA, citing concerns about the agency's role in perpetuating the refugee issue and its failure to promote peace. Despite this, other nations, particularly in Europe and the Arab world, continue to support the agency, seeing it as an essential lifeline for Palestinian refugees.

Beyond the issue of refugee status, critics argue that UNRWA's broader role in the conflict is one that sustains the conditions of war rather than alleviating them. While the agency provides much-needed humanitarian aid, such as education, healthcare, and food assistance, it has not addressed the deeper structural issues that contribute to the conflict. UNRWA's focus on emergency relief, rather than long-term development and reconciliation efforts, has led some to question whether the agency is truly contributing to peace or simply maintaining the status quo of suffering and division.

In contrast to UNRWA's approach, many have called for a new direction—one that focuses on reconciliation, empowerment, and sustainable development. Rather than perpetuating the refugee status of successive generations, there is a growing call for the integration of Palestinians into the societies in which they live. Countries such as Jordan, Lebanon, and Syria, where large numbers of Palestinian refugees reside, should be encouraged to create pathways to citizenship and self-reliance for these populations. At the same time, efforts should be made to improve the conditions in the West Bank and Gaza, fostering a sense of hope and opportunity for Palestinians, rather than reinforcing the rhetoric of displacement and victimhood.

Despite the controversy surrounding UNRWA, it is important to recognize that the agency was created in response to a genuine humanitarian crisis, and its continued provision of aid to Palestinian refugees remains essential. The problem, however, lies in the fact that UNRWA has not adapted to the changing realities of the conflict, and in doing so, it has become entangled in the politics of the Israeli-Palestinian dispute. The failure to promote a more comprehensive peace process, one that involves all parties acknowledging each other's legitimacy and moving beyond the narrow lens of victimhood, has prevented the agency from fulfilling its broader mandate of fostering lasting peace and stability.

As the conflict drags on, the international community faces an urgent need to reassess its role in resolving the refugee issue. The path forward will require a concerted effort to move away from the politics of victimization and towards a framework that prioritizes mutual recognition, respect, and compromise. Only then can the cycle of displacement and conflict be broken, and a more hopeful future for both Palestinians and Israelis be achieved. However, for this to happen, organizations like UNRWA must evolve and adapt their approach, working not only to alleviate immediate suffering but also to foster a long-term vision for peace, security, and coexistence.

Chapter 11: Conclusion - The Path Forward

The Israeli-Palestinian conflict, despite decades of international efforts, remains largely unresolved, with the central issue being Palestinian rejection of peace. This longstanding refusal to accept Israel's right to exist, combined with a steadfast denial of the legitimacy of the Israeli state, has been the primary obstacle to peace. Every attempt at peace talks has been undermined by this refusal, and each time, both the Palestinian and Israeli peoples bear the consequences of this intransigence.

As Shimon Peres, Israel's former president and Nobel Peace laureate, stated:

> "Peace will not come through hatred or violence. It will only come when both sides recognize each other's right to live in peace and security. Until that day, we will continue to face the consequences of rejectionism."

Peres' words reflect the harsh truth: the rejection of Israel's right to exist is a denial of peace itself. The lack of mutual recognition has meant that peace, thought possible, remains elusive.

Gabriel Zaliasnik, a prominent Chilean Jewish leader, captured the heart of the issue, pointing out the toll of rejection:

> "The path to peace is not easy, and it will not come without compromise. But the rejection of peace, as we have seen time and time again, only prolongs the suffering of both the Palestinian and Israeli people."

Zaliasnik's statement underscores that the failure to embrace peace has consequences for both sides. The continued refusal to engage in meaningful negotiations results not only in the perpetuation of conflict but also in the suffering of innocent people on both sides of the divide. If peace is to be realized, the cycle of rejection must be broken.

Gideon Sa'ar, Israel's Minister of National Security, has made it clear that Israel's willingness to negotiate peace hinges on the recognition of its right to exist:

> "Israel has always been willing to sit at the table for peace, but it requires partners who will recognize Israel's right to exist, who will denounce violence, and who are committed to building a better future for their people."

Sa'ar's statement emphasizes that Israel has repeatedly shown a willingness to pursue peace. However, this willingness can only be reciprocated when Palestinian leadership recognizes Israel's legitimacy and denounces violence. Without these essential steps, negotiations cannot progress.

Aviv Gur, an Israeli journalist, argued that denial is an obstacle to peace, writing:

> "We cannot afford to ignore the fundamental truth: peace will not come through denial. The history of the conflict teaches us that the way forward is built on acceptance, compromise, and a commitment to making this land a place of coexistence and opportunity for both peoples."

Gur's observation highlights the critical importance of shifting the narrative. Denial of the legitimacy of the other—whether Israel's right to exist or the Palestinian right to self-determination—fuels the conflict. Peace will remain out of reach unless both sides are willing to accept the other's identity and work toward coexistence.

Pilar Rahola, a Spanish journalist and political commentator, also pointed out the unsustainable nature of rejectionism, saying:

> "The rejection of peace is not a sustainable strategy. Eventually, the Palestinian leadership will have to accept the reality of Israel's existence and engage in meaningful negotiations."

Rahola's insight is crucial. While Palestinian leadership's rejection of peace may serve immediate political goals, it is not a long-term strategy that will lead to prosperity for the Palestinian people. Real peace can only be built through recognition, dialogue, and compromise.

Tony Blair, former British Prime Minister and an active participant in peace negotiations, also weighed in on the broader consequences of rejectionism, stating:

> "The rise in antisemitism after the Hamas attack on Israel is a stain on our societies. We cannot allow this form of hatred to fester under the guise of political disagreement. Antisemitism must be unequivocally rejected, and we must work together to combat this poison wherever it appears."

Blair's words underscore the destructive impact of rejectionism on the global stage. The Palestinian leadership's rejection of Israel's existence directly contributes to rising antisemitism around the world, fostering hatred and division far beyond the Middle East.

Ricardo Brodsky, a Chilean political analyst, criticized the international community's failure to address Palestinian rejectionism:

> "There is a double standard in how the international community treats the conflict. Palestinian rejectionism is rarely addressed, and the

leadership continues to be coddled, despite their refusal to negotiate peace."

Brodsky highlights a significant problem: while Israel is often pressured to make concessions, the refusal of Palestinian leadership to negotiate or recognize Israel's right to exist is largely ignored. This inconsistency in the international approach only prolongs the conflict and prevents a genuine solution from emerging.

Max Colodro, a Chilean political commentator, also pointed out the need for true leadership from both sides:

> "Peace requires leadership that is willing to transcend political calculations and focus on the future. Unfortunately, we have not yet seen leaders on both sides who are willing to take that leap for the sake of their peoples."

Colodro's remark speaks to the importance of visionary leadership. True peace can only emerge when both Palestinian and Israeli leaders transcend their political calculations and focus on the long-term benefit of their people. Until this happens, the conflict will remain unresolved.

Nayib Bukele, President of El Salvador, echoed the need for pragmatic leadership:

> "We need leaders who will prioritize the well-being of their people, not their own political survival. This means making tough choices, including compromises, for the sake of a lasting peace."

Bukele's words call for courage and sacrifice from leadership. Peace requires making difficult decisions, and Palestinian leadership must be willing to make those decisions, even if it means compromising on long standing positions. Only through such willingness can a sustainable peace be built.

Looking back to the early Zionist thinkers, Theodor Herzl, the father of modern political Zionism, recognized the need for peace and cooperation with the surrounding Arab populations:

> "The Jewish state will have to seek the friendship of the surrounding peoples... We want peace with them, and they shall have it from us." (Der Judenstaat, 1896)

Herzl envisioned a peaceful coexistence with the Arab peoples of the region, a vision that has been thwarted by continued Palestinian rejectionism. His call for mutual recognition remains as relevant today as it was over a century ago.

Max Nordau, a leading figure in early Zionism, emphasized the importance of forging bonds with local populations:

> "We do not wish to conquer the land of others, but to redeem our own. We wish to live in peace with our neighbors, but we will not abandon our right to live freely in our own homeland."

Nordau's words reinforce the Zionist ethos of seeking peace, not conquest. However, peace is impossible without mutual recognition, something that Palestinian leadership has persistently refused to offer. Until this fundamental right is acknowledged, peace remains an unattainable goal.

Ahad Ha'am (Reuven Remez), a prominent Zionist thinker, also emphasized the importance of Jewish cultural and national survival alongside peaceful relations:

> "The Jews must not only reclaim their land but must also live in harmony with the Arab peoples, for peace and mutual respect are the true path to the survival and flourishing of the Jewish people."

Remez's emphasis on coexistence and cultural preservation stresses the notion that peace cannot be achieved through force alone but requires understanding, respect, and cooperation.

Leon Pinsker, an early Zionist thinker, emphasized self-reliance and recognition in his seminal work Auto-Emancipation (1882):

> "The Jewish people must be strong and united. Only through our own efforts can we secure our future."

Pinsker's vision of a secure and independent Jewish homeland underscores the importance of Israel's right to exist—something that Palestinian rejectionism consistently denies. Until this fundamental right is acknowledged, peace remains an unattainable goal.

Isaac Herzog, the current President of Israel, has firmly stated Israel's desire for peace:

> "Israel desires peace with all its neighbors, but peace cannot come through violence or by denying the existence of Israel. The Palestinian leadership must choose the path of recognition."

Herzog's statement highlights the core of the conflict: peace will never be possible if Palestinian leadership continues to reject Israel's existence. Without recognition, there can be no meaningful dialogue, and thus no peace.

Finally, the President of AIPAC has emphasized that the path to peace lies in mutual recognition and the acceptance of Israel's right to exist:

> "The foundation of peace in the Middle East must be built on the acceptance of Israel's legitimacy. Only by recognizing Israel's right to exist can we move forward toward a lasting peace."

The President of AIPAC's statement underscores the necessity of recognizing Israel's legitimacy as a precondition for peace. Without this recognition, no amount of diplomacy or negotiation can bring an end to the conflict.

World Jewish Congress President, Ronald S. Lauder, has also spoken about the role of rejectionism in obstructing peace efforts:

> "It is time for the international community to recognize that until Palestinian leadership acknowledges Israel's right to exist, no real peace can be achieved. The failure to do so prolongs the suffering of both peoples."

Lauder's statement adds another layer to the argument: until the Palestinian leadership takes the necessary step of acknowledging Israel's legitimacy, peace cannot be anything more than a distant dream. The refusal to do so is a significant roadblock, not just for Israel, but for the Palestinians as well.

Shareen Hazkel, a prominent Israeli-Jewish leader, also emphasized the importance of peace and recognition in the pursuit of a lasting resolution:

> "Only when Palestinian—are willing to embrace the jews right to exist and reject violence, will be eventually a window of opportunity for peace

Denying and options for violence and terror
Long story of rejection and hate

Palestinian Terror Attacks: Murders, Kidnappings, and International Terrorism

The pattern of Palestinian violence against Jews stretches far beyond isolated incidents, representing a long-standing strategic approach aimed not only at Israeli military and political targets, but at the general civilian population. The frequency and brutality of terror attacks, kidnappings, and murders have grown to define much of the modern Palestinian struggle, deeply rooted in a narrative fueled by religious, political, and ideological motivations that are inseparable from deeply entrenched antisemitism. These acts, while often painted as responses to political oppression or occupation, reflect a broader and dangerous ideology that seeks to erase Jewish presence from the Middle East.

Terror Attacks and Murders

From the early stages of the Israeli-Palestinian conflict, terrorism against Jews has not been limited to sporadic acts of violence but has evolved into systematic campaigns of terror. One of the most significant periods of escalation came during the Second Intifada (2000–2005), a violent uprising against Israeli control of the West Bank and Gaza. During this period, Palestinian militant groups such as Hamas, Palestinian Islamic Jihad (PIJ), and Fatah's Al-Aqsa Martyrs' Brigades carried out a series of deadly suicide bombings, shooting sprees, and assaults on civilian targets. The goal of these attacks was not just to harm Israeli soldiers but to inflict maximum civilian casualties, sending a message to Israel that no place or person was safe. This shift to targeting civilians in crowded public spaces was emblematic of the growing radicalization within the Palestinian ranks, where Jewish civilians were now seen as legitimate targets.

A shocking example of this wave of terror was the 2001 Dolphinarium discotheque bombing in Tel Aviv, which killed 21 Israeli teenagers. The attack, carried out by a Hamas operative, was designed to strike at the heart of Israeli youth culture, causing not only casualties but also deep psychological trauma. Lesley Klaff observed, "The selection of civilian targets, especially young people, marked a deliberate strategy to break Israeli resolve and instill a sense of insecurity that transcends the battlefield." These attacks aimed to destabilize Israeli society, both physically and mentally, by making civilian spaces as dangerous as military zones.

The infamous Munich Olympics massacre in 1972, where Black September, a Palestinian terrorist group, kidnapped and murdered 11 Israeli athletes, was another pivotal moment in the history of Palestinian terrorism. This was one of the first major international acts of Palestinian terrorism, and it served as an early indication of the reach and persistence of Palestinian violence. As Michael Ehrlich argues, "The attack on Israeli athletes at the Munich Olympics served as a turning point in Palestinian terrorism, highlighting its global ambitions and the willingness to use any means necessary to advance the cause."

Kidnappings and Hostage Situations

The tactic of kidnapping and holding hostages has been a central component of Palestinian terrorism. Kidnapping serves as a form of leverage in negotiations and an opportunity to embarrass Israel on the international stage. Palestinian terror groups have frequently taken Israelis hostage, demanding the release of prisoners in exchange for their freedom. This was especially evident during the 2006 kidnapping of Gilad Shalit, an Israeli soldier who was captured by Hamas in a cross-border raid. Shalit was held captive in Gaza for over five years, and his situation became a major political issue in Israel, eventually resulting in a controversial exchange deal where over 1,000 Palestinian prisoners were released in exchange for his freedom. This deal raised significant questions about the Israeli government's priorities, as the release of prisoners with blood on their hands was seen by many as a concession to terrorism. Lesley Klaff remarked, "The kidnapping of Gilad Shalit and the subsequent negotiations underscored the high stakes of Palestinian terrorism and the emotional toll it takes on Israeli society."

Kidnapping has become a staple tactic for Palestinian factions, not only to extract concessions from Israel but also to keep the pressure on the Israeli government. The 2014 kidnapping and murder of three Israeli teenagers—Naftali Fraenkel, Gilad Shaar, and Eyal Yifrach—by Hamas militants exemplified this strategy. The teenagers were abducted while hitchhiking in the West Bank, and their bodies were found weeks later. The murder of these teenagers was a direct result of the incitement to violence that permeates Palestinian society, and it was a deeply symbolic attack. It targeted not only Israel but the sense of security that Israeli citizens had in their everyday lives. As Michael Ehrlich commented, "The kidnapping and murder of these three young men represented the normalization of violence in Palestinian culture, where human lives are seen as expendable in the service of ideological warfare."

Terrorism and Antisemitism: The Ideological Underpinnings

At the heart of these attacks lies a deeply ingrained antisemitism that views Jews as an enemy to be eradicated, not simply a political adversary. This belief is not merely a byproduct of the Israeli-Palestinian conflict, but rather a reflection of broader ideological narratives that have been developed and propagated within Palestinian society. As Bernard-Henri Lévy observed, "The Israeli-Palestinian conflict has often been framed in terms of religious and political warfare, but at its core, it is about the rejection of Jewish legitimacy in the region." Palestinian leaders, particularly those from Hamas, have long promoted this ideological stance, blending religious rhetoric with nationalist fervor. Hamas's founding charter explicitly calls for the destruction of Israel and the obliteration of Jews, asserting that "the Day of Judgment will not come until Muslims fight the Jews."

This pervasive ideology is bolstered by the Palestinian Authority's educational system, media, and political discourse, which repeatedly demonizes Jews as "invaders" and "oppressors." Palestinian children are often taught to view Jews as subhuman, a narrative that dehumanizes them and justifies violence. As Lesley Klaff notes, "The normalization of antisemitism through media and education systems contributes to a generation of young people who see terrorism as a legitimate form of resistance."

The impact of this indoctrination cannot be overstated. Einat Wilf explains, "Palestinian violence is not just about military occupation; it's about confronting Jews as a people, reinforcing a narrative that pits Palestinians against Jews not merely for land, but for the very legitimacy of their existence." This mindset perpetuates a cycle of violence that is rooted in a rejection of Jewish identity and history in the region.

Palestinian Incitement and Antisemitism

The role of incitement in perpetuating Palestinian terrorism is critical. Palestinian leaders, particularly from factions like Hamas and the Palestinian Authority (PA), regularly engage in rhetoric that glorifies violence and demonizes Jews. From official speeches to popular songs and media broadcasts, the message of hatred is pervasive. The Palestinian Authority's state-run television regularly airs content that portrays Jews as malevolent, manipulative figures who are bent on subjugating Muslims.

In 2018, Palestinian Authority President Mahmoud Abbas made a speech in which he claimed that Jews were responsible for the Holocaust, citing ancient religious texts to accuse them of misdeeds and justifying violence against them. Such rhetoric is not isolated, but part of a broader campaign to paint Jews as evil and irredeemable. This pattern of incitement has been widely condemned by international human rights organizations but continues to be an integral part of Palestinian political discourse.

The role of Palestinian terror in spreading antisemitism is evident in the attacks and violence that have come to define much of Palestinian resistance. Whether through the targeting of civilians or the incitement to hate, Palestinian terrorist groups have not only engaged in political warfare but have sought to fuel a deep-seated hatred of Jews that transcends the immediate conflict.

Conclusion: The Cycle of Violence and Hatred

Palestinian terrorism, with its devastating toll on both Israeli civilians and the broader Jewish community, reflects more than just a struggle for land—it is a continuation of a deeply ingrained hatred and an ideological campaign rooted in antisemitism. These acts of violence, whether bombings, kidnappings, or murders, are not simply political moves but are deeply tied to the rejection of Jewish identity and history in the region. Lesley Klaff highlights that, "At its core, Palestinian terrorism is driven not just by a desire for political sovereignty, but by a hatred of Jews that seeks their annihilation."

The perpetuation of this violence, along with the indoctrination of young Palestinians to view Jews as the ultimate enemy, has created a vicious cycle of violence. Until Palestinian leadership and society at large confront this deep-seated hatred, the path to peace will remain elusive. The Palestinian commitment to a culture of violence, combined with the rejection of Jewish rights to self-determination, ensures that the cycle of terror will continue to reverberate through the region for generations to come. The eradication of antisemitism from Palestinian society, alongside a genuine recognition of the Jewish people's right to exist, is crucial for breaking this cycle of hatred and violence.

The ongoing and glaring inconsistency in the treatment of Israel on the global stage reflects an alarming and deep-rooted antisemitism that affects the very fabric of international law and relations. Israel, as the only Jewish state in the world, is frequently held to a different standard by various international bodies, including the United Nations (UN), the International Criminal Court (ICC), and other influential institutions. This unequal and antisemitic treatment ignores Israel's legitimate security concerns, often framing it as a uniquely aggressive and oppressive state despite its repeated efforts at peace and coexistence.

The Multilateral Institutions and Their Disproportionate Focus on Israel

The role of multilateral institutions such as the United Nations and the International Criminal Court (ICC) in their treatment of Israel has been a subject of considerable and reasonable critics . In these settings, Israel has faced disproportionate criticism, while other countries with far worse records on human rights and security, such as Syria, Iran, and North Korea, seem to evade similar scrutiny. This discrepancy has sparked condemnation from many world leaders who have called out the double standards that undermine the credibility of these institutions.

Global Leaders Speaking Out Against Bias

Amid this ongoing bias, numerous global leaders have rallied behind Israel, demanding fair treatment and calling for the reform of multilateral institutions. Their voices underscore the importance of a balanced approach to Israel's rights and its role on the global stage. These statements, from figures across the political spectrum, reflect a unified stance against the unfair targeting of Israel and the need for justice in international diplomacy.

Einat Wilf, former member of the Knesset and a prominent Israeli politician, has been an outspoken critic of the double standards applied to Israel at the United Nations and other international platforms. She said:

"Israel's right to defend itself against terrorism and to live in peace and security is non-negotiable. The international community cannot continue to single out Israel while turning a blind eye to the far worse human rights abuses happening in Syria, Iran, and other regions."

Avigdor Lieberman, Israel's former Minister of Defense, has consistently pointed out the hypocrisy in how Israel is treated in global forums. Lieberman remarked:

"There is a clear double standard when it comes to Israel. Multilateral institutions often fail to hold other nations accountable for their actions, while Israel, a democracy, is unjustly targeted. We must stand up against this systemic bias."

Joe Biden, President of the United States, has repeatedly voiced his strong support for Israel, reaffirming its right to exist and defend itself against external threats. Biden has been a vocal critic of the attempts to delegitimize Israel in international organizations. He said:

*"The United States stands with Israel, and we will continue

A practical example of antisemitism in the Treatment of Israel

The relentless and disproportionate focus on Israeli leaders, such as Prime Minister Benjamin Netanyahu and Defense Minister Yoav Gallant, within international legal and political frameworks is an explicit example of antisemitic bias. Alan Dershowitz, a distinguished legal scholar and advocate for Israel, has long criticized the focus on Israeli actions as part of a broader legal warfare aimed at delegitimizing Israel. In his view, the ICC's focus on Israel's self-defense measures, such as military actions in Gaza or against Hezbollah, is selective and politically motivated. As Dershowitz puts it, "Israel is the only country in the world that has been consistently and unjustly singled out for prosecution in international courts, while regimes like Iran and Syria, responsible for far greater crimes, are not even mentioned in the same breath."

This critique has been echoed by Gabriel Zaliasnik, a Chilean public figure and lawyer, who stated, "What is happening with Israel is a reflection of the kind of antisemitism that has been perpetuated under the guise of human rights. Israel is held to an impossible standard while its enemies are allowed to thrive, and that is no coincidence." Zaliasnik's comments emphasize the double standard applied to Israel in both legal and political spheres, wherein the Jewish state is condemned for defending itself, while states and groups that sponsor terrorism and commit genocide remain untouched.

In the political realm, leaders like U.S. Congress member Richie Torres have expressed their strong opposition to this double standard. Torres, a staunch advocate for Israel's right to exist and defend itself, has remarked, "To single out Israel for condemnation while ignoring the actions of brutal dictatorships like Iran and Syria is not just a diplomatic error—it is an act of antisemitism." His criticism points to the hypocrisy inherent in international politics when it comes to Israel's treatment. Torres' perspective aligns with the views of many pro-Israel organizations such as AIPAC (American Israel Public Affairs Committee) and the Anti-Defamation League (ADL), both of which have consistently condemned the targeting of Israel and called attention to the broader implications of such actions. The ADL has warned that the "disproportionate targeting of Israel is a modern manifestation of antisemitism, and it fuels the delegitimization of the Jewish state in ways that are both dangerous and harmful to peace."

13 International Bodies and Israel's Disproportionate Treatment

One of the most striking examples of this double standard is found within the United Nations. The UN has passed more resolutions condemning Israel than all other nations combined. These resolutions often criticize Israel for defending itself against terrorist organizations, such as Hamas, which has openly called for Israel's destruction. However, the same UN body has consistently failed to hold regimes responsible for far worse atrocities, such as Iran's sponsorship of terrorism and Syria's use of chemical weapons against its own people. The UN's inability to hold these regimes accountable underscores the hypocrisy at the heart of its approach to Israel.

The UN's actions were harshly criticized by Gabriel Zaliasnik, who stated, "When you have the UN General Assembly condemning Israel for defending its citizens, while at the same time allowing the participation of dictatorships like Iran and North Korea, it is a reflection of the international community's antisemitic bias, where Israel is punished for defending itself and its right to exist." This criticism is consistent with the broader narrative shared by pro-Israel advocacy groups, including AIPAC, which regularly highlights the double standard Israel faces at the UN. AIPAC's statement on this issue asserts that "The UN's continued focus on Israel at the expense of holding actual human rights abusers accountable undermines the credibility of the institution and fosters a climate of injustice."

Ignoring True Atrocities: Iran and Syria

While Israel faces harsh condemnation from international bodies, regimes responsible for far greater human rights abuses are largely ignored. Iran, under the rule of Ayatollah Khamenei, is a prime example. Iran has been a leading sponsor of terrorism, providing funding, training, and arms to groups like Hezbollah and Hamas. Iran's government has also engaged in systemic human rights abuses, including the execution of political dissidents, the suppression of women's rights, and the brutal crackdown on peaceful protesters. Yet, Iran faces little to no international accountability. As Alan Dershowitz has pointed out, "Iran's leaders have openly called for the destruction of Israel, and yet the ICC does nothing. This is the kind of selective enforcement that destroys the integrity of international law."

Similarly, Syria's President Bashar al-Assad has been responsible for the deaths of hundreds of thousands of his own citizens through chemical warfare, bombings of civilian areas, and the targeting of hospitals and schools. Yet, Assad remains unchallenged by the international community, which has failed to apply the same legal rigor to his crimes as it has to Israel's defensive actions. As Bernard-Henri Lévy, a prominent French philosopher and advocate for human rights, has stated, "The fact that Israel is held to such a different standard, while the atrocities of regimes like Assad's go largely unpunished, shows the bias and antisemitism at the heart of international law and politics."

The Role of Advocacy Groups: AIPAC, ADL, and Political Leaders

Advocacy groups such as the ADL and AIPAC have been vocal in their defense of Israel, drawing attention to the deeply ingrained antisemitism that underpins much of the criticism directed at the Jewish state. AIPAC's efforts have been instrumental in ensuring that Israel's right to self-defense is recognized and respected in U.S. and global politics. The ADL, for its part, has consistently denounced the false equivalency drawn between Israel's defensive actions and the crimes of authoritarian regimes. The ADL's national director, Jonathan Greenblatt, has said, "To single out Israel for criticism is to ignore the basic right of every country to defend itself. When Israel is held to a higher standard than any other country, it is a form of antisemitism that has no place in international law."

Moreover, political figures like Richie Torres have continued to push for a balanced approach to the Middle East, insisting that "Israel is the only democracy in the Middle East, and it should be treated as such, with respect for its right to exist and protect its citizens." His position is in line with the broader sentiment within the Jewish community and Israel's allies, who believe that global institutions must stop applying a biased set of standards to the Jewish state.

Centrist Senator Susan Collins and openly pro-Israel Democrat John Fetterman have both voiced their disagreement with the arrest warrants. Fetterman shared a headline about the decision on X, captioning it, "No standing, relevance, or path. Screw that."

Additionally, Argentine President Javier Milei joined in denouncing the warrants, stating on X that his nation "expresses its profound disapproval" of the decision, which he claimed "disregards Israel's right to defend itself against ongoing assaults from terrorist groups like Hamas and Hezbollah."

Czech Prime Minister Petr Fiala criticized the ruling, asserting that "the ICC's regrettable decision undermines its authority in other matters by equating the elected leaders of a democratic nation with those of an Islamist terrorist organization."

Hungary's Foreign Minister Peter Szijjártó also condemned the ICC's ruling as "shameful and absurd." He stated during a conversation with Foreign Minister Gideon Sa'ar, according to a Hungarian official summary, "This decision discredits the international judiciary by equating the leaders of a nation that has suffered a horrific terrorist attack with the leaders of the terrorist organization responsible."

Conclusion: The Need for Fairness and Justice

The treatment of Israel within the global arena reveals a disturbing trend of antisemitism disguised as a concern for human rights. The constant and disproportionate condemnation of Israel, coupled with the failure to hold authoritarian regimes accountable for their far worse crimes, undermines the integrity of international law and justice. As Leslie Klaff, a legal academic, has noted, "When Israel is demonized and held to a different standard, it perpetuates the myth of the 'other' Jew, a stereotype that has plagued the Jewish people for centuries." This selective justice not only isolates Israel but also damages the credibility of international institutions, such as the ICC and the UN, by showing that they are willing to turn a blind eye to true human rights abuses while focusing their ire on Israel.

As long as Israel is treated differently from other nations—held to a higher standard because of its Jewish identity—global institutions will continue to perpetuate antisemitism in the guise of diplomacy and human rights. True justice can only be achieved when all nations are held to the same standard, and when Israel's right to exist and defend itself is respected by the international community.

—-

Chapter 14: The Global Surge of Antisemitism Post-October Pogrom

: A Global Crisis

The horrific Hamas attack on October 7, 2023, which resulted in the deaths of over a thousand Israelis and the wounding of many more, marked a tragic turning point in the ongoing Israel-Palestine conflict. This attack not only shocked the world due to its scale and brutality but also set in motion a frightening global surge in antisemitism that has been felt in communities across the globe, from Europe to North America, Latin America, and beyond. The attacks were not merely an isolated military conflict but a catalyst that ignited a resurgence of violence and hatred against Jews, Israelis, and those perceived to be sympathetic to Israel. This chapter explores the global implications of this rise in antisemitism, illustrating how it has manifested in violence, discriminatory policies, and political rhetoric, while also examining the dangers it poses to Jewish communities worldwide.

Violence and Aggression: A Worldwide Surge in Antisemitic Incidents

In the aftermath of October 7, antisemitic violence quickly spread across the world. Europe, with its large and historically significant Jewish communities, saw an alarming rise in attacks. In France, Germany, and the United Kingdom, violent incidents escalated almost immediately. Jewish schools, synagogues, and businesses were attacked in numerous cities. In some cases, protestors chanting anti-Israel slogans crossed the line into antisemitism, attacking Jews simply because of their religious or cultural identity. France, which has faced tensions surrounding its Muslim and Jewish communities for years, saw violent demonstrations where Jewish properties were vandalized, and Jewish people were targeted in street attacks.

This pattern of violence was not limited to Europe. Canada saw an uptick in hate crimes directed at Jews, and the United States was no exception. On American university campuses, particularly those in New York and California, students and faculty members openly expressed support for Hamas and Palestinians, but in doing so, they often crossed the line into openly antisemitic rhetoric. Jewish students were harassed, and in some cases, even physically attacked. Jewish symbols were defaced, and the atmosphere on campuses became increasingly hostile for those who stood in solidarity with Israel.

In Latin America, while many countries took a more neutral stance, the Palestinian cause had gained significant traction in recent years, and the aftermath of October 7 revealed a growing tolerance for antisemitic rhetoric. Governments, such as those in Chile and Argentina, saw demonstrations that blurred the lines between criticism of Israel and outright antisemitism. In Chile, for example, the Seret Israeli Film Festival was canceled due to threats from pro-Palestinian groups, marking a rare and worrying instance of cultural and artistic expression being suppressed due to the fear of violence. In Argentina, Bolivia, and Nicaragua, public officials made statements that resonated with antisemitic tropes, condemning Israel without distinction between the actions of Hamas and the broader Jewish community.

The global surge in violence and the increasingly hostile climate towards Jews are not mere coincidences. They represent a larger trend that can be traced back to decades of antisemitic rhetoric gaining ground, both in political spaces and on the streets. The normalization of these extreme attitudes was accelerated after October 7. Rather than coming together as a global community to condemn the terrorist attacks, many countries, particularly those in the Middle East and parts of Europe, allowed antisemitic conspiracy theories to flourish unchecked.

The Political Rhetoric: Governments and Leaders Contributing to Antisemitism

While violence is the most visible form of rising antisemitism, political rhetoric has played an equally significant role in enabling its spread. Governments around the world, either through direct action or through their silence, have contributed to this global wave of hatred.

In Europe, several governments and political leaders have been accused of tacitly supporting antisemitism through their failure to act decisively in curbing hate speech and violence. In Spain, Ireland, and the United Kingdom, government officials have made statements that some critics argue have emboldened antisemitic actors. The Spanish government, for instance, faced widespread criticism when it failed to explicitly condemn an attack on a Jewish institution in Barcelona, and Ireland experienced a surge in anti-Israel sentiment, with some factions of the government using the Israel-Palestine conflict as a vehicle for advancing their political agenda, often at the expense of the Jewish community.

In Chile, President Gabriel Boric's administration faced significant pressure after his government was slow and doubting to unequivocally condemn rising antisemitic violence and rhetoric. The Seret Israeli Film Festival, an event showcasing Israeli culture and cinema, was canceled due to threats from pro-Palestinian groups who warned of violence if it went forward. This incident became a flashpoint in the debate over antisemitism in Chile, revealing the challenges of maintaining cultural neutrality in a time of geopolitical conflict. Although Chile's Jewish community had been an integral part of the nation's history, the political climate post-October 7 made it increasingly difficult for Jewish organizations to safely operate in public spaces without facing threats.

In Latin America, a similar dynamic unfolded, with pro-Palestinian protests spilling into antisemitic rhetoric. Leaders like Bolivia's Evo Morales, Nicaragua's Daniel Ortega, and Chile's Boric have historically aligned themselves with the Palestinian cause, but have, in some cases, ignored or even tacitly supported the rise of antisemitism. They have been absolutely ambiguous regarding the use of terrorism like a political tool , and they have beeb irresponsible with their own countries? adopting an anti zionist speech, that is basically to embrace an antisemitic agenda. The rhetoric espoused by these leaders often fed into the broader narrative of delegitimizing Israel, creating an environment where extreme ideologies could take root, unchecked by clear opposition or condemnation from government institutions.

The Role of International Organizations: Failing to Address the Root Causes

Perhaps the most troubling aspect of the global rise in antisemitism post-October 7 is the failure of international organizations to address the root causes and implications of this hatred. The International Criminal Court (ICC), for example, issued a warrant for the arrest of Israeli Prime Minister Benjamin Netanyahu and former defense minister l Israeli Yoahv Galant, accusing them of war crimes related to the conflict in Gaza. While the ICC's actions were purportedly aimed at holding individuals accountable for their actions, the decision was widely seen as an extension of antisemitic bias—a political move that unfairly targeted Israel without acknowledging the broader context of Hamas' violence and the larger threats to Jewish people worldwide. European Union officials and others within the United Nations have failed to strike a proper balance in their statements, often allowing antisemitism to fester in public discourse while condemning Israel in sweeping terms that do not distinguish between legitimate critique and incitement to violence.

A Global Crisis: The Return of Dangerous Ideologies

What we are witnessing is not merely a brief moment of unrest but a long-term, systemic rise of antisemitism that mirrors dark chapters in history. The 20th century, particularly in the years leading up to the Second World War, saw similar patterns—waves of antisemitic rhetoric and violence that sought to delegitimize Jewish life and ultimately led to horrific consequences. The parallels between the pre-war period and what is happening today are chilling. In the 1930s, Jewish communities were increasingly isolated, politically and socially marginalized, and blamed for societal problems. Today, we are seeing historic analogies play out with increasing frequency: the public dehumanization of Jews, an environment ripe for the spread of conspiracy theories, and violent hate crimes erupting in major cities across the globe.

We must also recognize that, while the international community has voiced condemnation of Hamas' terrorist acts, it has been remarkably slow in condemning the broader antisemitic backlash that followed. The failure to directly address antisemitism—whether in the Middle East, Europe, or Latin America—only serves to embolden those who seek to use violence and rhetoric to attack Jews and Israelis worldwide.

As history has shown, silence is complicity. Governments and international bodies must not remain passive in the face of this rising tide of antisemitism. By failing to take meaningful action, we risk allowing history to repeat itself. As Zionist leaders from David Ben-Gurion to Golda Meir and beyond have emphasized, the establishment of the State of Israel was not only a political victory but also a statement about the right of Jews to live freely and safely in their own homeland. But that right is only meaningful if Jewish people can live safely wherever they are—not just in Israel, but in New York, Paris, Buenos Aires, and Santiago.

Chapter 15

Hamas is Palestinian, and Palestinians are Hamas

The tragic reality that many in the world refuse to acknowledge is the uncomfortable truth that even leaders such as the President of the United States have mistakenly attempted to distinguish Hamas from the Palestinian people. This flawed perception has dangerous implications. For over 16 years, the Palestinian Authority has avoided holding elections, fully aware that they would lose to Hamas. This avoidance of democratic processes is not just a political tactic; it reflects the deeper ideological and political reality that Hamas enjoys significant support among Palestinians. Particularly in Gaza, the disturbing pride in the violence of October 7th, when Hamas carried out a horrific attack, is a direct reflection of the underlying political sentiment. As Sharren Haskel, a member of Israel's Knesset, asserts, "Peace is not achievable through territorial concessions; we must focus on security, and security requires sovereignty."

Haskel's view highlights the stark contrast between the international community's calls for concessions and the deep-seated reality on the ground. Palestinians in Gaza, especially, have shown no hesitation in aligning with Hamas's radical ideology. This is not an isolated phenomenon but a reflection of the prevailing sentiment within the region, with many Palestinian factions displaying open pride for acts of violence against Israel. Michael Ehrlich points out, "The reality is that Hamas has always been a reflection of the broader Palestinian society, especially in Gaza. The Palestinians in Gaza have shown no signs of abandoning Hamas, and in fact, most support it in one form or another."

This unfortunate reality complicates the international community's ability to address the conflict effectively. The distinction between Hamas and the Palestinian people is, in many ways, an illusion—one that prevents the world from grappling with the full scope of the challenge at hand.

Here's the expanded version with additional context and analysis:

—-

Sharren Miriam Haskel: The Security Imperative

Knesset Member Sharren Miriam Haskel is unwavering in her stance that any peace efforts involving Israel must prioritize security over territorial concessions. She argues that the principle of land-for-peace has consistently proven unrealistic, particularly given the Palestinian leadership's refusal—especially by groups like Hamas—to recognize Israel's right to exist. Haskel explains, "The road to peace is paved with the recognition of Israel's right to exist, and we cannot achieve this through appeasement."

Haskel's perspective is rooted in Israel's historical experiences, where territorial compromises have frequently led to increased threats rather than peace. For instance, she points to the 2005 withdrawal from Gaza, which was intended as a step toward peace but resulted instead in Hamas taking control of the area and using it as a launching pad for rocket attacks against Israeli civilians. "We've seen what happens when security is compromised in the name of peace: it's not peace that follows, but war," Haskel warns.

She also critiques the international community's tendency to pressure Israel into concessions without holding the Palestinian leadership accountable for its rejectionist policies. "We must acknowledge that the Palestinian leadership has, for decades, reinforced a culture of hate. Acknowledging Israel's right to exist must be the starting point, not just a temporary concession." Haskel emphasizes that peace can only be built on a foundation of mutual recognition and security guarantees.

Einat Wilf, a former Knesset member and scholar, complements this viewpoint by addressing the deeper cultural and ideological challenges to peace. She explains, "Peace is not the result of negotiations; it is the result of a fundamental shift in mindset. Without recognition of Israel's right to exist as a Jewish state, no agreement will hold." Wilf argues that the educational systems and media narratives within Palestinian society must stop perpetuating hatred and denial of Israel's legitimacy. "A future of coexistence starts in the classroom, not at the negotiating table. Teaching children to hate ensures that the next generation is primed for conflict, not peace."

Aviv Gur, an Israeli security analyst, further contextualizes these issues by emphasizing the strategic implications of prioritizing security. "Israel's security is not just about protecting its citizens; it is about preserving the values of democracy and freedom in a region hostile to them," he explains. Gur points to the destabilizing effects of territorial concessions, warning, "Territorial concessions made under duress or false promises of peace have historically led to greater instability. The lessons of Gaza should never be forgotten."

Mr. Wilder from the Netherlands adds an international perspective, highlighting Europe's role in fostering or hindering peace. "Security is not a luxury for Israel; it is a necessity dictated by its environment. Any peace process that ignores this will be doomed to failure," Wilder states. He calls on Europe to stop pressuring Israel into concessions that undermine its safety, instead advocating for policies that challenge extremist ideologies. "Europe's moral responsibility is to support Israel's right to defend itself against existential threats, not to pressure it into making concessions that compromise its survival."

—-

Juan Flores: Psychological Insights into the Conflict

Juan Flores, a Chilean psychologist specializing in conflict resolution, brings a psychological lens to the discussion, arguing that unresolved collective trauma is a significant barrier to peace. Flores explains, "When collective trauma remains untreated, it manifests as a continuous cycle of aggression and victimhood, which prevents real progress toward peace." Both Israeli and Palestinian societies bear deep scars from decades of violence, and Flores contends that addressing this trauma is essential for sustainable peace.

In Palestinian society, this trauma is compounded by years of indoctrination into narratives of victimhood and resistance. Flores notes, *"True leadership involves confronting past tra

About the Author

Daniel Alejandro Farcas Guendelman

Biographical sketches

In 1992, he obtained the President of the Republic Scholarship to pursue postgraduate studies in Spain, where he specialized in Business Administration at the Institute for Executive Development in Madrid. Later, he pursued a Ph.D. in Leadership in Higher Education at Capella University, United States[1]Between 2002 and 2010, he was vice president and prorector of the University of Arts, Sciences and Communication (Uniacc) and rector of the IACC Professional Institute. Since his arrival in Israel in the year 2021 he has been an associate professor at Bar Ilan University During the government of President Eduardo Frei Ruiz-Tagle, he was appointed director of the Division of Social Organizations (DOS) and held the position of national director of the National Training and Employment Service (SENCE), during the government of President Ricardo Lagos Escobar. Legislature 2014-2018Deputy of the Party for Democracy for District No. 17, Metropolitan Region, period 2014-2018